KISSING

A BIG SKY NOVEL

Jenna

NEW YORK TIMES BEST SELLING AUTHOR

KRISTEN PROBY

A Big Sky Novel
Kristen Proby

Cover Art:Photography by: Sara Eirew Photographer
Cover and Formatting Design: Uplifting Designs

Print interior photo credit: Trevon Baker

ISBN: 978-1-63350-032-7

Published by Ampersand Publishing, Inc.

ACKNOWLEDGEMENTS

I need to send out my sincerest gratitude to Gail Goodwin, the owner, artist and entrepreneur who owns Snow Bear Chalets in Whitefish, Montana. I'd always known that Jenna Hull was a fierce businesswoman, and that she would be the innkeeper that Christian fell in love with. But when I saw Ms. Goodwin's tree houses, I knew that they were Jenna's passion, as well. What a perfect place to fall in love.

Gail, your willingness to answer my unending questions, and your generosity in inviting me to the tree houses for research were invaluable while I was writing this book, and I am forever grateful. But more than that, I've found a new friend, and that's the best part of all. Thank you for everything.

Dear reader: If you're interested in visiting the real life tree houses, called Snow Bear Chalets, please visit www.snowbearchalets.com.

Other Books by Kristen Proby

The Big Sky Series

Charming Hannah
Kissing Jenna
Waiting for Willa - Coming Soon

Kristen Proby's Crossover Collection – A Big Sky Novel

Soaring with Fallon
Wicked Force: A Wicked Horse Vegas/Big Sky Novella by Sawyer Bennett
All Stars Fall: A Seaside Pictures/Big Sky Novella by Rachel Van Dyken
Hold On: A Play On/Big Sky Novella by Samantha Young
Worth Fighting For: A Warrior Fight Club/Big Sky Novella by Laura Kaye
Crazy Imperfect Love: A Dirty Dicks/Big Sky Novella by K.L. Grayson
Nothing Without You: A Forever Yours/Big Sky Novella by Monica Murphy

The Fusion Series

Listen To Me
Close To You
Blush For Me
The Beauty of Us
Savor You

The Boudreaux Series

Easy Love
Easy Charm
Easy Melody
Easy Kisses
Easy Magic
Easy Fortune
Easy Nights

The With Me In Seattle Series

Come Away With Me
Under the Mistletoe With Me
Fight With Me
Play With Me
Rock With Me
Safe With Me
Tied With Me
Breathe With Me
Forever With Me

The Love Under the Big Sky Series

Loving Cara
Seducing Lauren
Falling For Jillian
Saving Grace

From 1001 Dark Nights

Easy With You
Easy For Keeps
No Reservations

Tempting Brooke

The Romancing Manhattan Series

All the Way - Coming Soon

KISSING

A BIG SKY NOVEL

Jenna

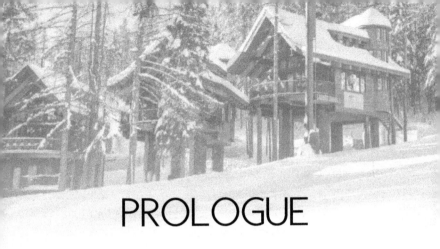

PROLOGUE

Christian

"**D**O YOU HAVE YOUR shit figured out?"

Luke Williams is sitting across from me in a restaurant in downtown Seattle, where he summoned me a week ago. I just flew in this morning, on his private jet, to meet with him. I cleared my full schedule for this.

No one in Hollywood says no to Luke Williams. Not if you want to succeed, that is. It seems Luke has the Midas touch when it comes to blockbuster movies, and I admit that I want to work with him. I've admired him for the better part of my life. Taking this meeting was a no-brainer.

"What shit would that be?" I sit back, my sunglasses still on my face, and take a sip of my room-temperature water with a squeeze of lemon. His blue eyes narrow as he watches me intently.

"I live in Seattle, not on Mars, Christian. People talk in our little world. I know you've had some challenges in the past few years."

Try since I was six.

Being a child-actor-turned-adult-super-celebrity isn't without its challenges. I've been smart enough to stay far away from the drugs, and most of the women. Hell, I've been Hollywood's clean-cut movie star for the majority of my life, and the image has done well for me. But being in this world means that you choose distance. Loneliness. And it suddenly occurs to me that Luke might be one of the only people in the world who would understand that.

He starred in some of the most successful movies ever made about a decade ago, and despite the mega-stardom, came out of it with a happy marriage and a career that the rest of us envy.

"I'm doing all right. I won an Oscar last year."

"Congratulations on that, by the way. You also got yourself a DUI and had a very public breakup with your girlfriend."

He's not smirking, he's just watching me while stating facts that anyone who reads a tabloid would know.

"I'm doing fine," I repeat and take off my glasses, tossing them onto the table, then pinch the bridge of my nose. "And I'm curious as to why you brought me all the way to Seattle, just to have lunch. So you could grill me about my very public private life? You could have just called."

I expect him to smirk, but he doesn't. He rubs his fingers over his lips before sitting forward. "You know, Christian, if you ever want to talk about anything, any of it, I'm here. I know you don't know me well, but you can trust me."

I believe him. Luke is fiercely private, and I trust that anything I were to say to him would remain between us. I could let my walls down with him, but I'm not sure that we're there yet.

"Thanks for the offer," I reply sincerely and push my hand through my hair. "I'm figuring things out."

He's quiet for a moment, then nods once.

"There's a movie that I'm producing. It's big-budget, and I think it could snag you another Oscar."

"You could have just called my agent."

"I could," he replies with a shrug. "But, I wanted to talk to you in person. This isn't an action movie like the ones I've been making the past few years."

I tilt my head, my interest piqued.

"This one is based on a true story. It's about a skier."

"Is there a book for me to read?"

His lips twitch now. "Of course, there's a book."

"I don't know how to ski," I warn him, but he just shrugs.

"That's fine. In fact, it might be good for you to get out of town for a while and prepare for the role, learn to ski, enjoy a change of scenery."

"I haven't taken the role yet."

"I hope you will," he says with a smile. He spends the next ten minutes selling me on the film, and when he's finished, he writes down a figure that makes even me swallow hard.

"That's a lot of money."

"This is a big deal," he replies and rests his hands on the table. "I know you need to talk to your agent and your attorney, but frankly, you're the only actor that I'm considering for this. I want you."

"Why?"

"You're talented. And I think you'll bring some grit to this role, an edge that it needs."

"I am gritty these days," I reply with a laugh.

"Which is better than the pretty boy you were as a teenager," Luke adds, making me narrow my eyes. "It's not easy to transition from a child actor to an adult one. I know that. But you're doing it, despite the bumps in the road."

"Thank you. I think." He smiles, and I find myself smiling back at him. "I guess I'd better start looking for a ski resort so I can get some lessons in."

"Excellent," Luke replies. "Just don't break a leg. I don't want to have to postpone filming."

"I'll do my best."

CHAPTER ONE

Jenna

L AST NIGHT WAS OFF the hizzy.

My beautiful tree houses, Snow Wolf Cottages, are finally finished and open for business. It took a year, several contractor changes, and more money than I anticipated, but here we are.

Thanksgiving weekend is just finished, and I waved my college buddies goodbye this morning as they drove down the hill to the airport, headed back to Port Hudson, New York, to take over the world with their uber-successful company, LWW Enterprises.

I couldn't be happier for them. And because they're proud of me, too, three of them came to Cunningham Falls, Montana, to celebrate the grand opening weekend for Snow Wolf Cottages with my local friends and family.

I hosted the party here in the largest of the

three units, and we partied into the wee hours of the morning when everyone went home, and the four of us college friends laughed until it was time for them to leave.

I already miss them.

I'm sitting on the snowy deck, wrapped in a quilt, my feet up on the banister and a steaming hot mug of coffee gripped in my hands, taking in the silence of the early morning on a mountain.

Whitetail Ski Resort is blanketed in soft powder, ready for ski season to open tomorrow. My tree houses sit right along one of the runs, and I'm excited for my guests to be able to watch the skiers zip by from the comfort of the luxurious accommodations I've provided them.

This is my soul project.

I wanted a place where people could come to visit my hometown of Cunningham Falls and be surrounded by absolute rustic opulence while falling in love with the charm of the area.

And then they'll go home and make room for someone else.

A deer meanders down the ski run in front of me, sniffing the air.

"Do you smell my coffee, sweet girl?" I ask softly, and she twitches her ears at me, then continues walking away.

Yes, this is where my heart is. This mountain. This town. These people.

I can hear tires crunching over the fresh snow before I see the sleek, black SUV turn the corner toward my place. It parks in the lot below my deck, and a man climbs out, walks around to the back to fetch his luggage, and then stops to take a deep breath and to take in the tree houses looming over him.

It seems Mr. Flint Stone is early.

I narrow my eyes, not moving, and take another sip of my coffee. He's not supposed to be here until later this afternoon, and I've always been a stickler for a schedule. But one thing I've learned while being in the hospitality business is that you have to be flexible.

Even if being flexible includes greeting a guest in my pajamas and bunny slippers.

The man waves and offers me a smile, and I wave back.

"Mr. Stone?" I call down.

Of course, that's not his real name, but he nods.

"Just climb that staircase," I point to my left, "and I'll meet you at the front door."

He nods, and I stand to go inside, shedding my quilt but not setting down my coffee. No, someone would have to pry it from my cold, dead hands.

I open the door and step back, inviting the stranger inside. "Sorry, this won't be your unit. I stayed here last night."

Christ, he's better-looking in person than on the

movie screen. He sets his bag down and brushes some snow from his dark blond hair.

"Hi," he says with a smile.

"Hi. I'm Jenna." He shakes my hand, and I'm surprised by how warm his skin is.

"Sorry I'm so early," he says. "The plane was ready, and I decided to take advantage of it."

"No worries," I reply with a shrug and hook my hair behind my ear. "I didn't think I'd ever meet a guest without makeup, in my pajamas and bunny slippers, but here we are."

He glances around the messy tree house with humor in his blue eyes. "Looks like you had a hell of a party."

"Oh, we did," I confirm. "That doesn't happen often, and I'd anticipated the mess being gone before you got here. This is my grand opening, and my friends helped me celebrate."

"Congratulations," he says as his eyes land on the mug I'm holding. "*I do not spew profanities. I enunciate them like a fucking lady,*" he reads with a smile.

"Damn right," I reply with a nod. "Now, let me grab my keys, and I'll show you to your very clean, very comfortable space."

"Thank you."

He doesn't move from the doorway as I walk into the kitchen and rummage in my handbag for the keys to his unit. When I return to him, his hands are in his pockets, and he's waiting quietly.

"This way, Mr. Stone."

His lips twitch with humor as I lead him from my unit to the one on the opposite end. "There are three tree houses, as you can see. I've put you in this end unit, called the Tamarack, named after the trees found on this property."

"This is beautiful," he says, looking around. "I don't know if I've seen anything quite like it."

"I know," I reply with a smile. "Trust me, you haven't."

I pass him my mug while I unlock the door, then retrieve it and lead him inside, flipping on lights as I go.

"Come on in. This is your home away from home for the next four weeks." I pause in the kitchen while he wanders through the space, looking outside, then taking in the blue kitchen cabinets, the large gas fireplace, and the comfortable furniture. "In the email correspondence, you asked for extra groceries to be stocked in the kitchen, and I've done that for you."

"Thanks," he says. "Where's the closest Starbucks?"

I lean my hip on the counter and take a sip of my now lukewarm coffee. "In town."

"Not on the mountain?"

"There's a coffee shop up here, yes, but it doesn't open until tomorrow when the season officially starts. I believe that's the case for the restaurants up here, too."

"So, no food up here?"

I shake my head. "No, but I'll take pity on you and make you dinner tonight, if you like."

His eyes narrow, suspicion written all over his face. "Why would you do that?"

I lean in as if I'm about to tell him a secret and whisper loudly, "Because I'm a nice person."

He doesn't smile.

"You can figure it out for yourself if you want to." I shrug and lead him to the barn door that closes the small bedroom off the living space. "This is the bedroom on this level. There's a bathroom here, too. I'll show you the upstairs."

I climb the stairs, certain that his eyes are on my ass, and hear him gasp when we reach the top.

"Cool, huh?"

"Beautiful," he murmurs again, looking up. There's a turret, accessible only by a ladder that has a bed and a blue ceiling covered in stars. I flip a switch, and the stars light up.

"I wired every one of those myself," I inform him quietly, sipping my coffee. "It was a pain in the ass."

"But so worth it," he says and smiles down at me. I can see why he's taken. He's handsome and well-spoken. As far as I can tell, he's charming.

His girlfriend, who was splashed all over *Peo-*

ple magazine last week, is a lucky woman.

"Thank you," I reply with a happy smile. "You'll have privacy here. And if you need anything, just give me a call. My number is on the kitchen counter, along with the Wi-Fi password. Oh, you'll find that your cell signal isn't great up here. It's better if you go out on the deck."

"That's not ideal," he says with a sigh and pushes his hand through his hair, but then shrugs a shoulder. "But we'll figure it out. I couldn't get UberEats to find any restaurants on my app earlier."

I laugh now, delighted with him.

"No UberEats in the boonies, Mr. Stone. But my offer for dinner tonight still stands if you like. I'll be in the Ponderosa unit again. You're welcome to join me."

He thinks it over for a moment and then nods. "I'd like that. Thank you."

"You're welcome." I lead him back down to the kitchen. "Well, I guess I'll leave you to it. Have a good day."

"Jenna."

I turn to see him standing there, tall and broad, his hands in his pockets again as he watches me with those wary blue eyes.

"Yes?"

"My name isn't really Flint Stone."

"I know." I open the door and then turn back

to him before shutting it behind me. "Have a good day, Christian."

The smirk on his face is the last thing I see before I close the door and walk back to the Ponderosa. Snow is falling again in huge, light flakes that stick to my eyelashes and hair.

I love it.

I walk into the tree house and sigh. Man, we did a number on the place last night. You'd think we were *back* in college.

I grin, ready to roll up my sleeves and get to work cleaning up.

It was so worth it.

***

"What are you doing?" I ask Max as I stir the pasta and keep an eye on the marinara I've had simmering all afternoon. I wipe my hands on my red apron as I shift back and forth between the boiling pasta and the simmering red sauce.

"Calling you," he says, his voice dry. "What are *you* doing?"

"I'm making dinner. I offered to feed my tenant tonight since the restaurants don't open up here until tomorrow."

"That was nice of you," he says with a sigh.

"Why did you just sigh like that?"

"Like what?"

"Like you're irritated or disappointed or something."

He laughs, and I put him on speaker and set the phone down so I can butter the bread with two hands. "I'm not any of those things. I just think you're too nice sometimes. It's not like she couldn't come to town to have dinner."

"It's a he," I reply absentmindedly.

"Come again?"

"Oh for fuck's sake, Max, it's not like he's a rapist or a serial killer or something."

"Who is it?"

"I'm not telling." I frown as I set the colander in the sink and dump the pasta, draining it. "I have an obligation to my guests' privacy."

"You're not a lawyer or a doctor."

"I still take it seriously, so I'm not telling you who it is. But don't worry, I'm fairly certain that I could do that Vulcan neck pinch thing or something if push comes to shove."

"Not funny," Max replies.

"Do *not* come up here and try to save me from something imaginary," I warn him, shaking my finger at the phone.

"I can't. I had to fly to California today."

Ironic. Christian came from California, and Max went there.

"How long will you be gone?" I ask.

"Just a few days. Week at the most. Will you

pick up my mail for me?"

"You seriously need an assistant."

"No, I don't, I have you," he says with a laugh, and I flip him off, even though he can't see it. "Put your finger away."

"Are you psychic?"

"Yes," he says. "Please grab my mail for me, and I won't call Brad and tell him to come up to the tree houses armed."

Brad is our police chief brother, and he'd absolutely do something like that.

"You wouldn't."

"Oh, try me, baby sister."

"You're a pain in the ass, Max Hull. But, of course, I'll get the mail. Am I going to have to chase a woman out of there this time?"

I can practically hear him cringe. He'd forgotten about the woman sleeping in his bed the last time he went out of town. She'd set up house in Max's place while he was gone.

Until I found her there and practically dragged her out by her long, red hair.

"Learned that lesson. Be careful, Jenna."

"Love you, too. Bye."

I hit end and turn around. "Holy shit!"

"Sorry." Christian holds up his hands in surrender. "I didn't want to interrupt your phone call. The door was open."

I brace my hand over my heart and catch my breath.

"Scared the hell out of me."

"I'm really sorry," he says and smiles cautiously. "And whoever that was is right. You should be careful."

"Gonna off me?" I ask and return to stirring the sauce. "That might be bad for your image."

He shoves his hands into his pockets, his blue eyes laughing. He's wearing the same jeans from this morning, but he changed into a grey sweatshirt that hugs his arms nicely.

"You could be right," he says. "You changed out of your pajamas."

I snort and check on the garlic bread toasting in the oven. "Of course, I did."

"I kind of liked them, but the black sweater works, too," he replies with a small shrug, his lips turning up with a grin. "How can I help?"

"I'm done here. I didn't know what you like, but I figured spaghetti is usually a sure bet."

"I did cardio today, so pasta would be great." He accepts a heaping plate from me and snags a slice of warm garlic bread, as well.

"I'm a casual girl. How do you feel about sitting in the living room?"

"Lead the way," he replies. We settle in the living room, him on the couch and me in the big rocking chair facing him. We eat in silence for a long minute, too busy chewing to talk.

"Why did you continue to call me Mr. Stone this morning, even though you knew that wasn't my name?"

"Hey, if you want to be Flint Stone, who am I to tell you that you can't be?" I take a bite of bread. "You booked the unit under that name, I assumed that's what you wanted to be called."

"My manager booked it," he says, looking down at his half-eaten meal. The muscles in his jaw flex as he chews.

Under different circumstances, I might be tempted to bite him there.

"She always books things for me under false names," he continues. "It's a running joke."

"It's pretty funny." I lick my fork and smile when I notice his eyes dilate as he watches me. "Do you like your space?"

"It's great," he says. "I admit, when she said I'd be staying at a tiny resort in Montana, I pictured it being much more—"

"Rustic?"

He nods.

"There are plenty of those places here, but I wanted to build something for people like me. I'm picky when I travel. I like to stay in nice places, but I also like to soak in the local charm."

"I'd say you hit the nail on the head with these," he says with a nod. "I know plenty of people who would rent these out."

"That's the goal, Mr. Stone." He laughs, and my stomach clenches. Christian Wolfe has a great laugh. "Word of mouth is the best marketing there is."

"Are these the only ones you own?"

"No, I have rental properties all over town. I just purchased a piece of property up in the national park earlier this year. Once the snow clears in the spring, I'm going to build one more tree house up there."

"An entrepreneur."

"Indeed."

"Are you originally from here?" he asks, and he seems genuinely interested. I'm enjoying the company, so I fill him in on my roots here in Montana.

"Yes, and I have two brothers. Max was the guy you heard on the phone. He's always in and out of here on business. And my other brother, Brad, is the police chief in town.

"We are fourth-generation locals."

"Wow," Christian replies. "That's cool."

"I think so, too. Are you from L.A.?"

A change happens now. A subtle shift. His body tenses, but he doesn't miss a beat in his answer.

"No, my family is from Tennessee, but we moved to L.A. when I was young."

It sounds like a recording. Like this is the answer he's been trained to give, over and over again.

"Do you ever go back to Tennessee?"

"Not often." He shakes his head.

"Can I ask you a question?"

He blinks rapidly and seems to steel himself for the onslaught of questions that I'm sure he gets every day.

"Okay."

"Do you want dessert? I made huckleberry turnovers with some leftover berries that I had in the freezer."

He blinks again. "That's the question?"

"Yeah. It's an important question, Christian. I don't want to eat it by myself."

"I don't think I've ever had huckleberries before."

"You're in for a treat," I promise him as I stand and take his empty plate and walk into the kitchen. "They're a local berry. I think they mostly only grow in the Pacific Northwest area. Their growing season is short, so we pick all we can in the summer and freeze them."

"I'd love to try them."

I turn to find him standing at the island, smiling at me.

"Do you want ice cream with it?"

"Of course."

"You're my kind of people," I say and take the

turnovers out of the warming drawer of the oven, scoop out the ice cream, and we settle in our spots in the living room again. "So, why a whole month here? Are you running from the FBI? The CIA? The IRS?"

"No," he says, laughing. "I'm going to learn how to ski for a movie role."

"That's cool, but you're athletic. I'm not going to lie, Christian, I've seen some of your movies. I'd guess that you could learn to ski in a week."

"I need to look like I was born on the slopes. Like it's second nature to me."

"Makes sense." I lick my spoon and nod. "So, you'll be spending a lot of time on skis."

"That's the plan."

"Do you have an instructor lined up? I know the owner of the resort if not, and he could set you up with someone excellent."

"Nina already arranged it."

"Who's Nina?"

His lips twitch. "My manager. And my sister."

"Ah, yes, I remember her name from her email." I set my empty plate aside and lean back, my belly blissfully full. "Good God, stick a fork in me."

"You fed us a lot of carbs."

"Comfort food." I shrug. "I didn't know what to expect with you."

"Same here." He stands, sets our plates in the

sink and stuffs his hands back into his pockets. "I should go. I'm meeting the instructor at six."

"In the a.m.?"

"That's the one."

"Yikes." I stand and walk him to the door. "Well, good luck tomorrow."

"Thanks for dinner." He stops in front of me and is so close I could lean in and kiss his chest. I can feel the heat coming off of him, and the thought of walking right into his arms and feeling him wrap around me sounds like absolute heaven.

But he's a stranger. He's famous. He's only here for four weeks.

And he has a girlfriend.

I clearly need to date more.

"Jenna?"

"Yeah?"

He laughs. "I said thanks for dinner."

"Oh, you're welcome." I wave him off and tuck my hair behind my ear. "See you later."

"Later." He winks and hurries away, and I'm left a quivering, lust-filled mess.

It's going to be a long month.

CHAPTER TWO

Christian

"**A**RE YOU TRYING TO kill me?" I join my instructor, Chad, at the bottom of the run and shove my goggles up onto my helmet, catching my breath. "This is the first day."

"You're a natural," he says and pats my shoulder. "You're way past the bunny hill, dude."

"I think that one was a black diamond," I reply and watch a couple of girls walk by, giving me the side-eye.

Yeah, it's me.

"And you handled it like a champ," he says. "We'll do one of those at the end of each day, and they get harder."

"Awesome."

Actually, it *is* awesome. The quiet, the cold, the snow. I've quickly discovered why skiing is so popular.

I've fallen in love with it in less than six hours.

"Let's go into the lodge before you leave," Chad suggests and pushes off on his skis, leading me to a huge building in the heart of the small village. "I want to introduce you to Bax. He owns the place."

Jenna mentioned him last night. I follow Chad, stepping out of my skis and swinging them up onto my shoulder to walk with him.

Once inside, I'm met by more people and the smell of freshly baked cookies, coming from the large tray sitting by the man-sized fireplace in the foyer.

"Bax," Chad says, and a man standing at the front desk turns to us. He's dressed casually in jeans and a North Face sweatshirt. "This is Christian."

"I knew it," a woman says from across the room, and I give her a wave with my signature grin, then turn my attention to the man before me, hoping that the fan and her friend don't come over for photos.

"Pleasure," he says. "I'm Jacob Baxter, the owner of Whitetail Mountain."

"The whole mountain?" I ask.

"Aside from the private residences, yes," he says. "The resort is mine."

He has a British accent, and I want to know all about how he came to own this resort in Montana, but I hold my questions. We're being watched, and most likely filmed, and I'd like to get back to the tree house.

"Thanks for loaning me Chad this month," I say. "He's awesome."

"He is," Jacob replies with a nod. "Let me know if you need anything. Are you staying nearby?"

"In Jenna's tree houses," I reply with a nod, and Jacob's head tilts. "What did I say?"

"Nothing, I'm just surprised my wife didn't say something. She's a fan and a good friend of Jenna's. I figured Jenna would have said something."

She just had Flint Stone on her schedule. But the fact that she hasn't called Jacob's wife since last night is interesting.

"Well, I'd be happy to say hello to your wife sometime."

Jacob smiles. "You're not working here, Christian. If she's around, that would be nice, but this isn't a photo op. My staff has been instructed to be cool. We get quite a few celebrities here, so it's not usually an issue, but I reminded all of them. However, I can't control the clients."

"I'm fine."

"You don't have security," Jacob replies quietly, his face sober.

"No," I admit and push my hand through my hair, then remember we're being watched and smile confidently. "I'll be okay. Thank you, though, for thinking of it."

"Let us know if you need anything." He turns to Chad. "Keep me posted."

"Yes, sir."

Jacob shakes my hand and then marches away, and I immediately lead Chad outside. Staying in one place too long invites people into your bubble.

Always stay on the move.

"I'm calling it a day," I say and offer my hand to shake. "Thanks again for today. Same time tomorrow?"

"We're going to have to push it back to seven," he says grimly. "I know we want to get most of the lesson in before we have a huge crowd, but the sun doesn't come up that early this time of year, and now that you have your gear, we'll hit the powder quickly."

"Seven it is, then. See you tomorrow."

I walk over to the tree house, glancing around to make sure that I'm not being followed, lean my skis in the area provided just inside, stow my boots, and shed the rest of my gear. I spent about two thousand dollars on all of this today, and I have to admit, it's pretty badass.

Speaking of badass, staying at a ski-in, ski-out place is convenient. This gear is heavy. I walk into the kitchen and immediately open the fridge for a bottle of water. I pop the top and guzzle it down before tossing the bottle into the recycle bin and reaching for another.

Skiing is done for today, but I still have an hour

workout ahead of me.

Staying in shape is vital. I've been a physical actor my whole life. Whether it be action roles, dancing roles, or even drama pieces that require me to show my body, I have to be in top physical condition.

I drop to the floor and easily pound out fifty push-ups, then turn over and do fifty sit-ups.

Take a sip of water and move smoothly into burpees.

The only downside of staying at a small resort is that there's no gym. The skiing works my legs nicely and is great cardio, but I have to work on my upper body, as well.

I'll have Nina send me dumbbells.

Speaking of Nina, I'm in a three-minute plank when my phone miraculously rings on the floor next to my elbow. Rather than risk dropping the call, I hit accept and put it on speaker.

"Hey."

"You're alive! Jesus H. Christ, Christian, I was positive you'd been eaten by a bear or fell off that mountain."

"And I'm the actor in the family," I mutter and sit, sipping my water. "I have shit reception up here. But I have Wi-Fi, so texts and email will work."

"Actually, that's perfect. I told you to go up there and relax, and if your phone isn't blowing up all the time, all the better. How is it?"

"Snowy. Cold. But the tree house is cool, and the people are nice so far."

"Have you been recognized?"

"What do you think?"

"Was it awful?"

"Actually, no. I got some looks, but no one approached me. It's pretty chill here."

"I'll cross my fingers that it stays that way," she says with a sigh. "I told everyone that you're preparing for a role, so it's pretty quiet here, too. But I have the team working your social media, and I'll make sure all correspondence goes through me. I'll just shoot you a daily email, and if something needs your immediate attention, I'll call."

"You know I love you, right?"

She scoffs into the phone. "Duh. What would you do without me?"

I have no idea. Having someone I trust to take care of things is vital. I'm lucky to have her.

"I need you to have some dumbbells sent here for me. I can do everything I need to except upper body. There are some cool ones on Amazon that I'll send you the link for."

"I'll order them today," she says, and I can tell by her voice that she's writing it down. "I'll text you when I have a delivery date."

"Thanks, Nina."

"That's what you pay me the big bucks for," she says with a laugh. "Have fun. Bone a snow bunny. Don't get her pregnant."

"*This* is your advice for my time in Montana?"

"It's good advice," she replies. "Relax while you're there. Make friends. Be a regular human being."

I roll my eyes. "I'll work on it."

"'Kay. Call me if you need me. I'll talk to you soon."

She hangs up, and I stand to drag my already sore ass up to the shower. *Be a regular human being.* I'm not sure that I remember what that's like.

And trust me, I'm not complaining. I have a life that people dream of. It doesn't suck.

But it *is* lonely. Calculated. Strategic.

I've had walls firmly in place since I was fifteen and found out the girl I had a crush on was only dating me because of the movie I'd just been in. She didn't want *me*.

I'm sure that's not always the case, and it happened when I was a kid. But it taught me a valuable lesson to keep my eyes open, and my heart locked up tight. To be friendly but not accessible.

I'm not starved for attention. I'm starved for connection.

I turn on the water, hot as it goes, and step under the stream. It pounds on my upper back, and I sigh in happiness. There's a hot tub out on the deck that I might use later tonight after all the crowds have gone home.

I immediately move into squats, a habit I'd formed years ago. I can get a hundred of them in before the shower's done. It's all about time management.

I've just stepped out and am drying off when I hear the doorbell ring.

"Fuck."

It's either a fan who followed me here or Jenna.

It better be Jenna.

I sling a towel around my waist and walk down the stairs to the door, look through the peephole, and smile when I see Jenna's sweet face staring back at me.

Cross-eyed.

I open the door and watch her jaw drop as her gaze automatically travels from my feet to my eyes. She swallows hard, then takes a sip out of the coffee mug in her hand.

I wish I was Felicia. She's always going somewhere.

I smirk at the funny mug and step back, ushering her in so I can shut the door and cut off the cold air.

"Sorry for interrupting," she says as she follows me to the kitchen. "I was about to go to town and thought I'd see if you were around and wanted to join me."

"What's up?"

"Well, you can't just be a hermit up here, no matter how pretty it is." She sits on a stool and sets her mug on the countertop. "I have a couple of errands to run, and I thought we could get a coffee at Drips & Sips. It's better than Starbucks."

"That's a bold claim," I reply and soak her in. She's fucking beautiful, and I've seen my fair share of gorgeous women. Touched them. Kissed them.

Made it look like I was fucking them.

Hell, I *did* fuck some of them.

But I don't know if I've ever seen anyone quite like Jenna. Maybe it's the gorgeous face, sexy figure, and long, blond hair mixed with the confidence. That doesn't happen often.

"Why didn't you tell your friend that I'm here?" I ask and watch her frown.

"Because that would be an invasion of privacy."

"So?"

Her brows climb into her hairline, and then she sips her coffee, watching me. "Well, I'm not a jerk. I can't just advertise who's staying at my place. That's not cool. Also, it's not my business to tell my friends that you're here."

"I met Jacob today," I inform her and lean on the counter. "He told me you're a good friend of his wife."

"Grace and I are good friends, yes," she says

with a nod. "And I know that she's a fan of yours."

"But you didn't call her."

"Christian." She takes a deep breath. "Like I said, it's not my place. If you told me it was okay, I would probably tell her, but I wouldn't volunteer the information.

"My brother is Max Hull. You may not know him—"

"The software genius?"

She nods.

"The one who sold his company to Google for like fifteen billion dollars?"

"I think it was just one billion," she says with a laugh. "But, yeah, that's the one. He isn't famous in the same way you are, but he has his challenges with it, too. And I am *fiercely* protective of him. I protect all of my clients in the same way. You're my client. And maybe my friend, but we'll see."

"I like you," I admit and then narrow my eyes. "Trust isn't easy."

"Not for most of us," she says with a shrug. "So, you don't have to join me today. You can tell me to go mind my own business, and you won't see me again until it's time to check out of here."

"I like you," I repeat, surprised to find that it's completely true. What I don't say is that I'm so fucking attracted to her, it may not be a good idea to hang out together because I want to bend her over this counter, and I'm only here for a month.

But along with that, I enjoy her company. Her quick wit.

And she's not an asshole.

"Let me get dressed, and I'll go with you."

"Yeah, don't wear the towel," she says, rubbing her chin as if she's thinking it over. "Famous or not, you'd draw a lot of attention, and I forgot to take a security class to keep the women off of you."

I smirk and shake my head, walking to the stairs.

"You're a smartass, Jenna."

"You're welcome."

***

Cunningham Falls is tiny. For a guy who grew up in L.A., it's the size of a postage stamp. But it's also quaint and quite beautiful.

"We have a few stoplights," Jenna says as she drives us into the heart of downtown. "Main Street is a whole three blocks long, so don't blink or you'll miss it."

She winks at me, and I want to reach over and tuck her hair behind her ear. So, I do. She glances over at me in surprise and keeps talking.

"We also have amazing restaurants and fun shops. We are definitely a resort town, but I don't think it's cheesy."

"It doesn't look cheesy."

"Believe it or not, winter is my least favorite

season," she says as she parks her SUV in front of Drips & Sips and cuts the engine, then turns to me. "I don't enjoy winter activities as much as I do summer. Construction is difficult in the winter, so much of my business slows down on that front. And, it tends to be long for us here because we sit in a valley so we're socked in a lot. By February, I'm longing for sunshine.

"But I can't deny that it's beautiful, especially before Christmas."

"You should be a tour guide for a living," I reply, and she laughs.

"I do know a lot about this town. If you ever have a hankering to know which houses are haunted, and who owns what, I'm your girl."

"I'll keep that in mind."

We climb out of her vehicle and walk into the coffee shop, and I immediately sweep the area, taking in the number of people, and how many of them look up to see us walk in.

There are two whose eyes light up when they see me, and I know they recognize me, but to my relief, no one makes any moves to rush over to us.

Jenna leads me to the counter where she orders a decaf mocha, and I order a chai tea latte. When our order is ready, we find a table in the back of the shop and sit, shedding our coats.

I sit with my back to the room.

Jenna smiles and takes a sip of her drink.

"Do you drink coffee all day?" I ask.

"Only until about two, and I cut off the caffeine at noon." She shrugs. "I know it's not great for me, but it's my one vice. I don't drink much, just when I'm with my girlfriends. I don't spend a million hours on social media. I work, and I drink coffee."

"That's it? No hobbies?"

"I do like to travel now and again," she says, then glances down and smiles at her coffee. "Oh, they made a snowflake in the foam."

She pulls her phone out and takes a picture, and I tense up. Her gaze whips up to mine.

"I just took a photo of the coffee."

"I know."

"I won't take your photo unless you say it's okay," she adds and slips her phone back into her pocket. "You've been screwed before, Christian."

"Oh, yeah."

"I won't do that."

Her voice is soft and sweet, and everything in me longs to believe her. I just met her yesterday, and I'm pulled to her in ways that surprise me. This doesn't happen. I don't *let* it happen.

"I hope not," I reply and take a sip of my tea. She laughs when I pull the cup away. "What?"

"You have foam on your lip." She leans over the table and wipes it away with her fingers, and I feel her touch all the way to the pit of my stomach. "There you go."

"Thanks."

"Do you want to walk around town a bit?" she asks. I don't want to wander out in the cold. I spent all morning in it. But I also don't want to go back to the tree house by myself, as stupid as that sounds.

I don't want to end the afternoon with her.

"No." I shift in my seat. "Is there a movie theater in town?"

"Of course." Her eyes widen. "You want to go to the movies?"

I nod, eager to sit in a dark theater with her, to watch magic happen on the screen as she sits next to me, munching on popcorn.

"Which one?"

"Any one."

She immediately pulls her phone out again and scrolls around for a moment, and I can't help but watch her fingers, remembering how they felt on my mouth.

I'm not going to be able to keep my hands off of her for long.

She checks the time. "They're playing the new *Star Wars* movie in thirty minutes."

"Let's do it. Unless you had other plans?"

"Nope. I like the movies." She smiles, almost shyly, and I can't help but reach over and smooth a lock of hair behind her ear again.

"Me, too." I stand, gather our empty cups, and wink at her. "Let's go."

CHAPTER THREE

Jenna

"HI," CHRISTIAN SAYS TO the young woman selling tickets at our small theater. Her brown eyes widen, and I think she might have just swallowed her tongue.

"Are you?" she stutters.

"Nah," Christian replies but then winks at her. She blushes. "Two for *Star Wars*, please."

She just nods and takes his cash, hands over the change, and then the poor thing walks over to the concessions counter to continue waiting on us.

"Are you sure?" she asks and bites her lip.

Christian just laughs and shakes his head. "I'll take a large popcorn and a bottle of water. How about you?" he asks me.

"Are you going to share your popcorn?"

"Absolutely not," he replies.

"A small one for me, then." I laugh and slip my hand through his arm, just in support. He glances down at me and smiles softly. It's interesting to watch his face harden in front of strangers when they recognize him and soften when he looks at me.

Is this what his life is?

"Would you like a drink?"

I blink, pulling myself out of my thoughts. "A diet Coke, please."

It's a quiet afternoon at our theater, which is good for us. We have our pick of seats when we walk into the auditorium, and Christian leads me halfway up and to the middle.

"This is the best spot," he says with a happy smile.

"I'm surprised you want to go to the movies." I sit beside him and take a bite of popcorn.

"Why?"

"It's like someone who works at McDonald's doesn't want to *eat* at McDonald's. They get sick of it."

"Not me." He shovels a handful of kernels into his mouth and chews loudly, making me giggle. "Love this."

"You're disgusting."

He opens his mouth, showing me his food, and I throw a piece of popcorn at his face, hitting him in the nose.

"Thanks," he says, plucking the kernel from his

shirt and popping it into his mouth, smiling as he chews. "What's your favorite movie?"

"*Steel Magnolias*," I reply immediately, and he scowls at me. "What?"

"*That's* your favorite?"

"Pink is my signature color," I reply with a deep southern accent. "It's a classic."

"Hmm. I might have to rethink this entire relationship."

"Okay, movie expert,"—that earns me a smug smile—"what's your favorite?"

He sighs and shoves another handful of popcorn into his mouth, thinking it over. God, he's something to write home about. That square jaw, the way his hair curls slightly over his earlobe. His muscular shoulders in that sweatshirt.

Sitting this close to him is bad for my libido.

"*Holiday Inn*," he says at last, and to say I'm surprised is an understatement.

"With Fred Astaire?"

"Yep." More popcorn is stuffed into his mouth.

"Why?"

He shrugs and takes a sip of his water. "Because the dancing is amazing. Old movies are magical. Innocent in a way. The talent is just out of this world. I can't imagine the number of choreography hours they invested."

I turn in my seat to watch him. I've seen him

dance on screen. Christian is talented in his own right.

"You're a good dancer."

He glances down at his popcorn. "Thanks. I enjoy it. I've always enjoyed everything about musical theater, the singing, the dancing. I trained for a lot of years."

"It shows."

"And I'm lucky that it comes pretty naturally to me."

"You *are* lucky. I have zero rhythm."

He scoffs and takes another drink of his water. "I don't believe that. Everyone has rhythm. We just have to find it."

I feel my eyes widen and shake my head. "I'm not dancing with you."

"Yes, you are."

"No."

"Come on." He nudges my shoulder with his. I look up into happy, blue eyes. "You're among friends."

Thankfully, the previews start, and I'm saved by darkness and advertising. We are the only ones here, in the dark, and the screen is a riot of color as we chew on our popcorn and enjoy the show.

I can't help but glance over at Christian and enjoy the emotion rolling over his face. His eyes never leave the screen. He's soaking it all in.

An alien jumps across the screen and I startle, letting out a squeak. Christian laughs and rests his hand on my thigh, patting me gently.

"You okay?"

"Yeah, damn alien."

He laughs again, and we're lost in the story once more. When his popcorn is gone, he reaches into my bag for a handful, brushing his fingers against mine.

Jesus, I feel the intensity of his touch down to the pit of my stomach. How can a simple touch ignite every nerve ending in my body?

And why does he smell so damn good?

I simply pass him the bag. I'm finished with it anyway, and I can't have him touching me like that. He has a damn girlfriend.

We're *just* friends.

Actually, we're acquaintances. He's a client. I'm a tour guide.

But damn, it doesn't suck to hang out with him.

And it has nothing at all to do with his celebrity status. He's funny. And sexy as hell. If he lived here and didn't have a girlfriend, I would ask him out.

I sigh, determined to focus on the movie and not on the irresistible man to my right.

When the credits finish rolling, we gather our trash and leave the theater, and once we're in my car, I turn to him.

"What did you think?"

"I'm still processing," he replies. "And I think you should have dinner with me so we can discuss it further."

I cock an eyebrow. "Are you asking me to dinner?"

"Yes."

"Because it sounded like a statement."

"Will you please have dinner with me?" He bats his thick, dark eyelashes and I can't help but laugh. I put the car in gear and pull away.

"Yes. As long as you're not tired of me."

"Definitely not. Maybe I'll get a couple of drinks in you and talk you into dancing with me."

"Not gonna happen."

No way, no how.

He just shrugs and watches the town pass by as we drive toward the mountain.

"What should we have for dinner?" I ask him.

"Not picky," he says.

"I have salmon and salad stuff in the fridge in the Ponderosa," I say, thinking aloud. "I think that's the last of my groceries up there."

"Do you live there full-time?"

"No, I've just been staying there for the past week or so, selfishly enjoying it now that the units are finished. I have a place in town."

He nods.

"Do you want to see it?"

"Your place? Sure."

I turn the corner and drive to my little house that's tucked away in an older neighborhood in town. I love it.

"I see my brother Brad came by to shovel," I comment as I pull into the garage and cut the engine. "Come on in."

Christian follows me into the house, walking close behind me. I can feel the heat of him.

I have permanent goosebumps from this man.

I flip on the lights in the mudroom, and then the kitchen.

"This is really great," he says, looking around the space. "You've remodeled."

"Of course, I have," I say with a laugh. "It's what I do. The house has been completely renovated, inside and out. But the original structure was built in 1904."

He glances over in surprise. "Wow, it doesn't look that old."

"I know." I sigh and rub my palm over the molding surrounding the doorway to the living room. "It did when I bought it. I had to replace the plumbing, the electrical, the roof. I did salvage the floors."

I glance up to see him watching me, his face completely sober. His hands are in his pockets, and he looks...*delicious.*

"Sorry, I'm rambling."

"It's your passion," he says simply, and I nod.

"Absolutely."

"Your face lights up when you're talking about your projects," he says and slowly walks toward me. I'm caught up in his eyes, unable to walk away. He stops about two feet in front of me and lifts his hand, drags his knuckles down my cheek. "You're a beautiful woman, Jenna Hull."

I swallow, my cheek buzzing from his touch. His eyes are on my lips now, and I instinctively lick them.

"Damn it," he mutters before he cups my face and neck in his hands. His lips are suddenly on mine, smooth and sure, taking me from quiet yearning to blazing fire in one-point-six seconds.

I grip his sides as he devours me. He nibbles the corner of my mouth, then plunders again as if he's memorizing every inch of me.

And, suddenly, a voice in my head reminds me.

He has a girlfriend.

I pull back, panting, wanting, and stare up at him as he also tries to catch his breath.

"Christian." He makes a move to go in for round two, and I press my hand to his chest. "No."

He stops immediately and pulls away, taking his hands completely off of me.

"I'm sorry. I didn't mean to start anything you're not comfortable with. I thought we were on the same page."

I push my hand through my hair and turn away to pace back to the kitchen.

"Oh, we're on the same page."

"Then what—?"

"You have a girlfriend," I blurt out and turn back to him, holding my hands out at my sides. "You're splashed all over every cover of every magazine, Christian. And I'm not the girl who poaches another woman's guy."

He shakes his head in frustration and braces his hands on his hips.

"She's not my girlfriend."

"I'm not blind."

"No. You don't understand." He looks as if he wants to lose his temper, but he rubs his hand over his lips and takes a deep breath. "Serena and I have to make it look like we're a couple for the media."

"That does *not* seriously happen."

"Oh, yeah, it does." He laughs without humor. "We're about to be promoting a movie that we co-star in, and the studio, along with all of the media, has coupled us up. But we're not seeing each other like that. I don't even really like her all that much."

"You're kidding." I cross my arms over my chest and stare at him in awe. "How can they do that?"

"It's not in our contract or anything, but we are expected to work the press junket. To walk the red carpets together. To look very much like a couple."

"Huh." I frown. "So, it's literally all an act."

He nods, his eyes sober again, and if I'm not mistaken, turn a little sad.

"The media lies about a lot of stuff. It sells magazines. It's not interesting to report the boring stuff. I work, I work out, I go home. That's not exciting."

"But your life is none of their business."

He looks as if he's going to laugh, but then he shrugs. "It doesn't matter."

"It matters."

I walk to him, and he watches me warily. I slip my arms under his and wrap them around him, pressing my cheek to his chest as I hug him tightly.

"I don't need you to feel sorry for me," he says, not hugging me back.

"Oh, please. You're a rich celebrity. I don't feel bad for you, I want to hug you."

He pauses a heartbeat and then wraps his arms around me to hold on fiercely. He presses his lips to the top of my head, and then I pull away.

I have to. Whether he's single or not, he won't be here for long, and he's not someone I should become attached to.

"Come on, I'll show you the rest of the house." I walk away but don't hear him following me. I pause and look back at him. "Are you coming?"

"Right behind you."

***

"You never told me what you thought of the movie," I say later when we're settled back up at the Ponderosa with our salmon and salad. We finished our tour of my house, then drove up here, and he went to his unit for a bit while I got dinner ready. He just arrived a few minutes ago.

So far, there's been no post-kiss awkwardness.

"It was pretty amazing," he says and takes a bite of his food. "Ron Howard directed this one, and there are usually specific things he does in his films that I wasn't sure if he'd do with this one, but I was pleasantly surprised to see that he did."

"Like what?"

"Well, he always casts his brother in a small part, and has since his first film, if I'm not mistaken. He also added a few other actors from previous movies that he's directed."

"So, like Easter eggs for diehard fans."

"Exactly. It was well done."

"Christian Wolfe approves." I take a sip of my wine. "I liked it, too. I didn't love the aliens. They're not attractive."

"I won't tell them you said that."

I stick out my tongue at him and keep talking. "I've enjoyed the prequel movies that Disney has done, but with this one, I'm not sure how they'll tie the story in with the rest of the series. I don't like that they're making the animated series relevant with the movie storyline."

He's stopped eating now, watching me with complete confusion all over his handsome face.

"You love *Star Wars*?"

"I have two brothers, Christian. Of course, I do. It's brilliant. And Han Solo has always been my favorite. I didn't know if they'd win me over with anyone other than Harrison Ford playing him."

"He's too old to play a twenty-something," he reminds me.

"He's Harrison Ford, Christian. He can do *anything*."

He laughs and holds up his hands in surrender. "True. Don't beat me up."

"I'm not violent." I sip my wine again. "It'll be interesting to see where Disney takes this."

He watches me thoughtfully and chews his dinner. When we're finished, he gathers our plates and sets them in the sink, then opens his phone. Before I know it, *Open Arms* by Journey is playing through the speaker. He sets the cell on the kitchen counter, turns to me, and crooks his finger.

"Christian, I can't dance."

"Just come here," he says and tilts his head in that adorable way he does when he's trying to charm me into something. He did the same thing when he suggested going to the movies today.

"Please."

I stand and cross to him, and he takes my hand, kisses my knuckles, and assumes the proper slow dance position.

"No means no," I remind him with a grin. His posture is ridiculously stellar. He's tall, and his arms are firm. His grip is confident, one hand on the middle of my back, and the other holding my hand.

"Just look into my eyes."

"I will break your feet."

His lips twitch with humor. "I hope not, I'm learning how to ski, remember?"

"I've warned you."

As Steve Perry's smooth voice fills the air, Christian moves us around the room. His body moves effortlessly, swaying with the music, and I just feel ridiculous.

Stiff.

"Outside my comfort zone." I bite my lip and look down.

"Up here," he says softly. "Just look at me. What fun is life if we always live it in our comfort zones?"

"I'm dancing with a famous guy in my living room," I remind him. "It's a little intimidating."

"I'm just a guy," he says and moves just a bit closer to me, tightening his grip. My nipples pucker in anticipation of being pressed against his chest.

"And no one is here but you and me, dancing to a pretty song."

"It is pretty," I concede. I can feel my body loosening now, moving with the music and drifting closer to him, lost in his eyes. "I haven't bloodied your feet yet."

"See? You're doing great." He kisses my forehead, and I feel myself softening more. My whole body is on high alert. My panties most likely soaked.

I like him. A lot.

"Not so bad, right?" he whispers against my forehead. He hasn't lost his posture, he's confident and steady.

"No, I can't say that this sucks." I feel his breath as he silently chuckles. "You're good at leading."

"You feel amazing," he mutters, and I clench my eyes closed. God, I'm so attracted to him. I don't think I've wanted anyone like this...*ever*. At least, not that I can remember.

Not that I can remember much of anything right now, as I stand here dancing in Christian's arms.

It feels like we're in a floaty bubble of lust and affection, and I don't want the bubble to burst. Even though I know it will, I just want to enjoy it for what it is.

I want to be in the moment with this sexy, likeable man and worry about the rest later.

The song has changed twice, and now P!nk is

crooning through the speakers.

"Did you put on only slow songs?" I ask him.

"Of course," he says. "It's not as much fun to dance like this to Metallica."

I snort out a laugh and brace my forehead on his chest, then look up at him and glide my hand from his shoulder to the back of his neck, enjoying the way his hair feels between my fingers.

He closes his eyes as though he's starved for touch, so I keep lightly scratching with my nails and let him silently sweep me around the room for three more songs.

Finally, I step into him and hug him close, the way I did at my house earlier.

"Thanks for the lesson."

His hands are firm against my back. "You're welcome. Maybe we should continue these lessons while I'm here."

I grin. "I mean, it would be silly to not take advantage of a professional dancer living so close to me."

"Exactly." He pulls back and smiles down at me, then stares at my lips again, but he doesn't kiss me.

He walks to the front door, slips on his shoes, and shoves his hands into his pockets.

"If I don't leave now, I won't leave."

Don't leave!

But it's too soon. So, I nod as if it's no big deal. "You probably have to get up early."

"Are you okay?" he asks.

"I'm so great." And it's completely true. "Sleep well, Christian."

"See you tomorrow, Jenna."

He winks and leaves, and I blow out a breath and fall onto the couch.

Holy shit, he's potent.

CHAPTER FOUR

Jenna

"MAN, I BROUGHT A lot of crap up here over the past couple of weeks," I mutter to myself as I stuff the last bag of my things into the back of my Toyota 4-Runner and pray that the door shuts.

"What are you up to, beautiful lady?"

I turn to find Christian approaching, his skis resting on his shoulder. He's in his gear, his hair messy and sweaty, and his chin stubbly.

I swear, he gets better looking every day, which is most likely impossible, but here we are.

"I'm packing up my car," I reply and internally high-five myself when the door closes without an issue. "I have a bunch of people coming over today for an open house-type party. My friend Penny is closing out a small business, and we always love an excuse to get together to chat and drink wine."

"That sounds fun," he says and rests his skis on the ground. "I haven't seen you in a couple of days."

It's true, it's been a couple of days since our dance lesson.

"I've been busy," I reply with a cringe. "I had an issue with a rental unit in town, and it required a lot of my time. It's fixed now, but I'm moving out of the Ponderosa for today's party and so I can start renting it out next week. I make too much income from these to keep them all to myself."

"How can I help?"

"You absolutely do *not* need to help. You're a guest."

I walk past him to the staircase that leads up to the front door, and I can hear him walking behind me.

"I'm here, and I'm available," he replies. "I'm happy to help. But I won't stay for the party."

I laugh as I turn the handle and turn to him. "No? You don't want to gossip, drink wine, and try on leggings?"

He swallows and frowns as if he's wondering how on earth I think that's fun, which only makes me laugh harder.

"It sounds like a girl thing."

"Totally a girl thing," I agree. "But I will take you up on a little prep work."

"Good." He drags his knuckles down my

cheek, and there's that buzzing in my skin again. "I've missed you."

"You're sweet."

"I'll go drop this stuff off and come back over to help."

"Thank you."

He winks, which seems to be his signature thing that makes me swoon more than I'm proud of.

I've just finished unloading the dishwasher and wiping down the clean countertop when he returns.

"How was your lesson today?"

"Great, actually," he replies with a nod. "I can see why so many people are addicted to skiing. It's an adrenaline rush for sure, especially when you catch air off one of the little cliffs and such."

"So I've been told," I reply and reach for a broom to sweep the floor. "I was never good at it. And then I had a friend lose her husband in a skiing accident a few years ago, and it just hasn't appealed to me since then."

"I'm sorry about that." He takes the broom from me and begins sweeping up the kitchen.

"I feel weird about you cleaning when you're a guest."

"I don't get to do this often," he says with a smile. "It's kind of fun."

"Well, you can stop anytime you want."

"Hey, Jenna! I'm a little early so I can set stuff

up before they get here." Penny comes hurrying in, carrying a big tote, not even looking our way. "I'm going to set this down and go get the other one. Be right back."

She marches right out again without sparing us a glance, and Christian and I share a smile. In less than thirty seconds, she's back, and then she sees Christian and comes to an abrupt halt.

"What the fuck? Did I take too many sleeping pills last night? I'm not sleeping, am I?"

"No," I reply with a laugh. "Penny, this is Christian. He's a guest here and has become a friend. Christian, this is Penny."

"Nice to meet you," she says and holds out her hand for his. She smiles, showing off a dimple, and then steps back and rubs her hands down her thighs. "Sorry for my language. I wasn't expecting, well, *you*."

"No worries." He waves her off and then turns to me. "If you guys have this, I'll head out."

"We have it," I assure him and walk him to the door. "Thanks for offering to help."

"I'll be about thirty feet away if you need anything." He kisses my cheek, and then he's gone, and I'm left with a *very* curious Penny.

"Christian Wolfe just kissed your cheek."

"Yep." I open her tote and begin pulling out clothes. "Where do you want these? Did you bring your rack thingies?"

"I don't give a shit about that," she says and props her hands on her hips. "Christian Wolfe had his hands on you. And if the way he looks at you is any indication, he wants to put more than that on you."

"Whatever." I snort and shake my head. "He's a guest. He's learning how to ski for a movie role. That's it."

"Uh-huh. Sure." She narrows her eyes. "Why did it have to be you? You never gossip."

I laugh louder and pull her in for a hug. "Let's sell all of these pretty clothes today, shall we?"

"See? You don't talk about the good stuff." She sighs and opens the other tote. "Everything is on hangers, so we'll just put them on the racks. They're down in my car, I'll go get them."

It only takes us about thirty minutes to get everything set up. I have plenty of appetizers and beverages to last into the evening, and it isn't long before our friends begin to show up.

Cunningham Falls is a small town, and many of us have been friends for a lot of years. Or, we're friends of friends. It's almost impossible not to be, and I admit that's one of the things that I love about living here.

Our community.

My brother Brad's fiancée, Hannah, arrives with our good friend Grace. They're both redheaded and beautiful, and Grace's pregnancy is just starting to show.

"I need all of the leggings," she says as she hugs Penny. Grace and Penny work together as teachers at the school. "My body is out of control, and literally *nothing* fits."

"I can hook you up, girl," Penny says as she leads Grace to a stack of colorful leggings.

"How are you?" Hannah asks me and takes a bite of a pita chip.

"Good. It's been a busy week. How are you?"

"Great." She smiles smugly. "Planning a wedding is both fun and infuriating."

"I can imagine. Just pass over a bunch of stuff to me. I'm happy to help."

"Oh, I will," she says with a nod. "And I have a question for you."

"Shoot."

"Well, I've been thinking. I asked my cousin, Abby, to be my maid of honor. Of course, Grace will be a bridesmaid because she's my oldest friend here." She reaches for my hand. "And I love you, Jenna. You're a great friend, and you're about to be my sister-in-law, and that just makes me so happy."

"Me, too. You're so good for my brother, and I love you, too."

"Will you be a bridesmaid?"

"Of course." I hug her tightly and then do a happy shimmy. "I'm so excited. We'll have to have a party with Grace, and maybe we can FaceTime Abby to go over plans."

"Actually, Abby should be in town before too long," she says, her blue eyes shining with excitement. "It sounds like she's going to be here for a while as a traveling nurse, so we can all get together in person."

"That would be so fun. Thanks for asking me."

"Thanks for saying yes."

At that moment, more friends file into the tree house, and I'm awash in happiness. I have wonderful people in my life.

Cara and Jillian King, best friends who married brothers, arrive carrying more wine.

"You are my people," I say as I hug them both and accept the wine.

"There's never enough wine," Cara says with a laugh. She's a pretty, petite blonde with the most gorgeous curves. I've always been jealous of her boobs.

I'm sorely lacking in that area.

"I can't have wine," Jillian says with a pout. "Zack knocked me up again."

"Congratulations!"

"All the pregnant girls are over here," Grace says, waving Jillian over. "Penny swears these leggings will fit us forever."

"Right on."

There's a knock at the door, and Lauren Sullivan pokes her head in. "Is this where the party is?"

"You found us," I reply and run over to hug her close. "And I've missed you."

"I know, I've missed you, too," she says and then pulls a book out of her bag. "I've been under some crazy deadlines. But I brought you a book so you can't be that mad at me."

"Thank you so much. You're forgiven."

Lauren writes amazing erotic romance novels, some of which have been made into movies. She's also sweet and quiet, and I adore her.

"Oh, good, you're here," Cara says, hugging Lauren.

I seriously love being part of a group of women who lift each other up rather than tear each other down.

"If anybody goes into labor, Hannah can handle it," Penny says with a laugh. Hannah is an OB/GYN in Cunningham Falls.

"We have months to go before that's an issue," Hannah assures us all and takes a sip of her Coke while admiring a pretty blue top. "How much is this, Penny?"

"I'll give it to you for twenty bucks," Penny replies with a shrug.

"Why are you closing all of this out?" I ask her.

"Well, I've decided to move," she says, and we all go quiet, looking at her in surprise. "I'm going to move in with a cousin in Seaside, Oregon."

"Why?" Cara asks.

"You guys, there's nothing for me here." She leans on the end of the couch. "The dating pool is a joke. I love my job, but even that feels...*stale*."

"I get it," Cara says with a nod. Cara is also a teacher at the elementary school. "It's not easy."

"I think I need a change of scenery for a while," Penny continues. "I love the ocean, and I don't really have anything keeping me here."

"But you can always come home if you need to," Jillian assures her. "Believe me, I know."

Jillian was gone for about a decade, living in California. She moved back to Cunningham Falls a few years ago and married her husband, Zack King.

"I know," Penny says with a nod. "I'm excited, you guys. But I need to sell all of this stuff."

"Well, we will help with that."

"Is anyone home?"

I turn to the doorway to find Willa smiling at me.

"Hey, girl! Come on in."

Willa Monroe is the owner of Dress It Up, a fabulous clothing boutique downtown. She's also someone I've known most of my life.

Max should have married her. My brother is an idiot.

"I'm so glad you're here," I say and loop my arm through hers. "There's food, booze, and clothes."

"All of my favorite things," she says with a laugh. "Alex is with my mom until tomorrow morning, so hook a tired mama up."

"You got it."

***

"Just so you know, I'm putting a Christmas tree in the Tamarack," I inform Christian the following day as he helps me unload Christmas decorations from my SUV.

"I don't need one," he says.

"*I* need one," I reply with a laugh. "I'm making the units beautiful for the holidays, so I'll be in there later, decorating."

"You can come in whenever you want."

I smile at him and pass him the last box. "Thanks. But I'll always give you a heads-up."

"So, what's in all of these boxes?"

"Lights. Ornaments. Garland." I set the box in front of the door of the middle unit, the Spruce. "I'm starting here because I have guests coming tomorrow, so I want to get it done first."

"Let's do it."

"Oh, you don't have to help me."

A slow smile slides over Christian's impossibly handsome face. "Jenna, I'm trying to find excuses to hang out with you. Haven't you figured that out yet?"

I swallow hard. "Why?"

"Because you're fun. Beautiful. You make me laugh." He tilts his head to the side and narrows his blue eyes. "Would you rather I didn't?"

"Nope, I just don't want you to feel obligated."

"There isn't much in this life that I feel obligated to do. Trust me when I say, I offer because I want to be with you."

And doesn't that just make a girl's stomach erupt with butterflies?

I move the boxes to where I want the coordinating décor in the rooms, and then fetch a ladder and get to work.

"What are you doing?" Christian asks.

"Hanging stuff." I frown down at him as I climb. "Can you please pass me the end of the garland?"

"Please come off the ladder."

His face is pale as he watches me.

"If I come down, who's going to hang this?"

"I don't give a fuck, I just don't want you up that high."

I slowly make my way back down and cup his face. "Are you afraid of heights?"

"Oh, yeah."

"But I'm not, and I'm the one on the ladder."

"It freaks me out," he says and tips his forehead against mine. "And that's not easy for me to admit."

"What about the ski lifts? Those are high."

"They're not ladders," he insists.

"I have to decorate. But I could probably hire someone to come and hang the high stuff."

"*I'll* hire someone if it keeps you off that ladder."

I want to delve into this particular conversation further, but there's a knock on the door.

"Jenna? Are you here?"

"That's Brad. In here!" I smile at Christian. "Come meet my brother."

"Lead the way."

We walk to the doorway, and I smile when I see that Brad brought Hannah with him. "Brad and Hannah, I'd like you to meet Christian Wolfe."

"Nice to meet you," Hannah says, shaking Christian's hand and then she winks at me.

"Are you staying here?" Brad asks, and I roll my eyes. Here we go with the big-brother thing.

"I am," Christian replies with a nod. "I was just giving Jenna a hand with the Christmas stuff."

"We brought the trees," Hannah says helpfully. "But I still say you should buy the trees I was telling you about on QVC. They're already decorated and everything. You just take them out of the box, plug them in, and *voilà!* Christmas tree."

"I need them to be fancier than that."

"Hey, I have one," Hannah says and then busts

out laughing.

"I had ornaments handmade for these trees," I say and then glance up at Christian, who's smiling down at me with sparkling, blue eyes.

What's he thinking?

"I don't need anything fancy," he says.

"Well, you're getting fancy because the other two are as well, and I need them all to match. Skiers see this, plus, I'm going to be featured in some travel magazines, and they have to look a certain way."

"She's very particular," Brad says with a wink. "But they're awesome, and she knows what she's talking about, so fancy they'll be."

"That's right." I nod once and then smile at the trees lying in the back of his big truck. "There's no way you're going to be able to haul those into these tree houses by yourself."

"He's not by himself," Christian says. "Do you have an extra pair of gloves?"

"I do," Brad says with a nod, and the men fall into step side by side, working on the trees.

"He's hotter in person," Hannah whispers beside me. I see Christian's lips twitch.

He totally heard her.

"You know," Brad says casually, as if he's talking about the weather, "I'm going to run a background check on you."

"Yeah? Why is that?" Christian asks.

"Because I see the way you look at her," Brad replies and holds up his hand to me, knowing that I'll interrupt. "And she's my sister. I don't give a shit who you are."

"Cool." Christian nods and helps Brad unload a second tree. "I can tell you in advance that I had a DUI about a year ago. It was stupid, and the press had a field day with it."

"I don't give a shit about the press either," Brad says.

"There's nothing else to find."

Brad nods, and when they've unloaded the final tree, he turns to Christian. "Do you plan to keep looking at her like that?"

"Oh, yeah."

Well, I guess that's good to know.

I look helplessly at Hannah, but she just shrugs and watches the two men with keen, blue eyes.

"Is this really happening?" I ask, but there's no response from either Christian or Brad.

"Don't be a dick," Brad says.

"Good advice," Christian replies, holds his hand out to shake Brad's, then rubs his palms together. "Now, where do these trees go?"

"Why are men like this?"

"Because we are," Brad replies and helps Christian lift a tree. "Now, show us where these damn things go. They're heavy."

"We're just friends, you know," I say as I lead the men into the unit and point to the corner of the living room. "We're not dating or anything."

"He's here," Brad says with a shrug that says he doesn't care.

"We've been on a date," Christian says with a scowl, and I make a cutting motion against my throat as if to say, *stop talking.*

"See?" Brad says.

"We're not a *couple.*"

"I mean, we went to the movies, I shared my popcorn with you—" Christian begins.

"You did *not* share your popcorn."

"And then we danced and everything. That constitutes a date."

"Oh my God, stop talking."

"Just saying," Christian says with a grin. "Brad, did you need my social security number for that background check?"

"That would help."

"I'm out of here." I roll my eyes and march past both of them, who are slapping each other on the back and laughing. "You're hilarious."

"I think so," Brad says with a nod.

"He barely kissed me," I continue, on a mini-rant now. "And we definitely haven't slept together."

"Yet," Christian says, his eyes full of lust.

"Okay, not funny anymore," Brad says. Hannah's hand is over her mouth, covering her laughter.

"Everyone out," I say, ushering them all to the door. "Let me work in peace."

Hannah and Brad both leave, but Christian stays behind, and I point my finger at him. "You, too."

"Me? Why me?"

"Because you're a troublemaker."

He smiles, shuts the door, and crowds me against the wall.

"I like your family."

I swallow hard and watch as he licks his lips.

"Well, that's nice."

"I'm going to kiss you, Jenna."

"Thank God."

CHAPTER FIVE

Christian

GOD, SHE'S BEAUTIFUL. Her chin is tipped up defiantly, but her blue eyes are screaming *kiss me right now!*

I rushed that first kiss. It took me by surprise, standing in her kitchen, how badly I had to get my hands—and my lips—on her.

I feel the same tug now, but there's no way in hell that I'm rushing it.

I step closer and cup her jawline in my hands, brushing the apples of her cheeks with my thumbs. Her skin is smooth, soft. She's pulled her hair into a knot at the top of her head, and wispy tendrils have fallen around her face, tickling the backs of my hands.

"You have little freckles across your nose," I murmur before leaning in to kiss her there.

"Too much sun," she whispers. I pull back to

look down at her, and her cheeks have flushed, her breathing is more ragged, and she's watching my lips as her tongue darts out to wet her bottom lip.

Fuck me.

I can't wait another moment. I tip her chin up with my finger and lay my lips over hers, breathing her in. She hitches one leg around my thigh in invitation, so I reach down, cup her ass, and boost her against the wall.

She wraps those legs around my waist, plunges her fingers into my hair, and holds on tightly as I plunder her mouth, tasting and nibbling, enjoying the hell out of her.

Jesus, I want her. More than I can remember ever wanting anyone in my life.

She makes a tiny mewling noise, turns her head, and gives me back as good as she gets. She's strong and sweet, and so fucking amazing.

"Jenna!"

I'm thrown out of the moment and pull back to stare into her confused, blue eyes.

"Who is that?" I ask.

"No idea," she mutters as I lower her to the ground. She opens the door of the tree house and walks onto the porch.

"There you are," a man says. "How are you, Jenna?"

"Good, thanks. What's up?"

I walk out with her. A man in a brown uniform

is hauling a box on a dolly.

"You usually receive deliveries at your house in town, so I was just making sure this is right before I drop it off. It's damn heavy."

"My weights," I say. "Sorry, I forgot to tell you that I had some dumbbells sent."

"No problem," Jenna says and then smiles at the deliveryman. "Looks like this is the correct place."

"Where do you want it?" he asks.

"I'll show you," I reply and lead him to my unit. "You can leave it here in the doorway."

"Sounds good," he says, then turns and whistles on his way back to his truck. Jenna is still on the porch. She waves him off then turns to me.

"I'm just going to unbox these real quick. I'll be back over in a few," I say, my voice rough with lust.

"I'll get some stuff decorated," she says with a nod, then waves me off and steps back inside.

I have to pause, take a deep breath, and will my libido to calm the hell down.

If we hadn't been interrupted, I would have fucked her against the wall, and that's not where I intend to take her for the first time.

It's going to happen, and soon. Keeping my hands off of her has been a form of torture I wouldn't wish on my worst enemy. And if the way she climbed me is any indication, the feeling is mutual.

But it's not going to be against the wall the first time.

Maybe the second time.

And this is not helping the hard-on I've got going on at all.

I pull my pocketknife out of my pocket and open the box, then pull the weights out and give them a once-over. It's a system from a popular exercise equipment company that makes it easy to lift anywhere from five pounds to seventy pounds, all in one dumbbell.

These are going to be perfect.

I set them up in the corner of the living room, then flatten the box they came in. When it's time for me to go back to L.A., I'll leave these behind for Jenna to keep here. Another guest might want to use them at some point.

I gather the box to throw away, then walk back over to the unit that Jenna's in, leave the box outside, and walk in without knocking.

She's just coming down off the ladder, and the garland is all hung.

"What are you doing?"

"Making it pretty," she says with a wink, then laughs when I just stare at her. "You were gone long enough that I could get this done so you didn't have to endure me being on the ladder."

"What happened to hiring someone?" I ask,

slowly walking toward her.

"I didn't need to," she says with a shrug. Her eyes light up as I get closer. "You look…intense."

"Oh, I am." She backs away, and I can't help but smile. "I'm intent on spanking your sweet ass."

"What?" She giggles and hurries away, putting the kitchen island between us. "You're *not* going to spank my ass."

"You were a bad girl." She laughs again, and my cock stirs. "Maybe I need to teach you a lesson."

She snorts. "Right, because I'm just supposed to fall in line with what the big, strong man said? In your dreams, pal."

She makes a run for the staircase, and I beat her there, pull her into my lap on the steps, and proceed to kiss her again, just as passionately as earlier. But now she's in my lap, practically sitting on my dick, and there's no one here to interrupt us.

"Does the idea of spanking me turn you on?" she asks and wiggles in my lap until she's straddling me, her pussy lined up perfectly with me.

"*You* turn me on, baby," I reply and return to kissing her silly.

"We're still strangers," she says but doesn't stop kissing me back.

"No, we're not." I rub a strand of her hair between my thumb and forefinger. "We're not strangers at all."

"It's fast." She tips her forehead to mine. "Is it too fast?"

"Does it feel too fast?"

She frowns. "No. It feels like I've known you a long time. And not because I've seen your face before this."

"I get it," I assure her. "I feel it, too."

I kiss her again, biting her lower lip. Suddenly, her phone rings, completely interrupting the moment.

"Shit," she whispers. "That's my brother's ringtone."

She pulls the phone out of her pocket, glares at it, then accepts the call.

"Hi, Brad."

"Hey," he replies. Jenna's so close to me, I can hear their conversation. "I just stopped by your house to check on things and shovel the driveway, and I have some bad news."

She frowns at me, not moving from my lap. "What is it?"

"Looks like a pipe froze and burst. You have water everywhere."

Her eyes close. "Fuck."

I pull her to me and hug her tightly.

"Looks like it probably ran through the night. I'm going to call a guy right now to start cleaning it up, I just wanted to let you know right away."

"Do you need me to come down there? I can be there in fifteen minutes."

"I don't think so. We'll get the water cleaned up and the pipe fixed. There's not a lot to do besides that."

"I'll swing by tomorrow morning," she says with a sigh. "Thanks for taking care of it, Brad. If I didn't have two groups coming in tomorrow, I'd come down right now."

"Take care of what you need to up there. I've got this."

They end the call, and she sighs. "Well, that's bad news."

"I'm sorry."

She moves off my lap and begins to pace.

"All of my units are full right now," she says, thinking aloud. "Which is good, but that also means that I don't have a place to stay while I have my house fixed. Actually, Max is out of town, so I could probably just crash at his house."

"Jenna."

She stops pacing and turns to me. "Yeah?"

"You can stay with me."

"No." She shakes her head. "You're a guest, and you're paying to be here. I'm not staying with you."

Why that irritates me, I'm not sure, but I pull myself up and walk to her. I've never felt the need to ask a woman to stay with me before. It's certainly not something I make a habit of. But I love that she treats me like any man that she recently met, and I definitely want to keep her close by for as long as I can. "I *want* you to stay with me."

She bites her lip. "It would be more convenient to be up here to welcome the guests."

"And I'll get to see you." I offer her my best grin, the one that's been splashed on dozens of magazine covers.

"It'll only be for a couple of days," she says.

"It's settled, then." I nod and reach for a box full of decorations. "Let's get this done so it's ready for your guests."

"Thank you."

I stop and look back at her. "You do realize that I have ulterior motives, right? We've been interrupted twice today, and I don't intend for it to happen again."

"Damn right," she says.

***

"So tired," she murmurs and stretches out on the small couch next to me.

"You should be tired." I kiss her head as she snuggles down and lays her head on my shoulder. "You worked your ass off."

She finished decorating all three units, stocked kitchens for incoming guests, and still managed to run down to her house to check on the status of things.

"It's no more than usual," she says and smiles up at me. "Wanna go up to the turret?"

"Sure."

She stands and offers me her hand, then leads me up the circular staircase to the loft. I've been using the king bed on the main floor, so I haven't been up here much since I arrived. There's another king-sized bed and a set of bunk beds along with another full bathroom.

Jenna starts to climb the ladder to the turret, which I don't love, and I reach for a couple of condoms in the bedside table.

I may not have been staying up here in the loft, but I was sure to stock the condoms on both floors, just in case.

A man can hope.

Jenna flipped on the tiny star lights in the ceiling of the turret and nothing else. I follow her up and climb under the covers of the king-sized feather mattress that is the only furniture up here and hold her against me, with just the glow of the stars shining down on us.

"How did you come up with this?" I ask her.

"A dream. I dreamed of these, and when I woke up in the middle of the night, I sketched it really quick before I forgot."

She glances out the window, then sits up in excitement.

"The sky cleared." She reaches over to turn off

the star lights. "Look."

I look out the window and catch my breath at the view of real stars in the sky.

"We don't get views like this in L.A."

"I know." She settles back against me again, and I'm spooning her now as we both watch the stars outside.

"Did it bother you, killing these huge trees to make the tree houses?"

"What do you mean?"

"They sit on enormous tree stumps. They must have been ancient trees."

She laughs and then turns to smile up at me. "They're not real. The center of them is steel, and I had them covered in fake tree bark, just like they use at Disney."

"Really?"

She nods and goes back to staring outside. "There weren't trees big enough to support a building like this, and I would never kill a tree that old. But I wanted them to look real, so I did research on what Disney uses in their parks to make the trees look real, and that's what I used."

"You're incredible," I whisper, leaning down to kiss her ear, then down to her neck. "I never would have thought of that."

"I'm a dreamer," she says and pulls my hand up to her lips. "And I'm a firm believer in making dreams happen. Now, at the risk of you not kissing my neck anymore, because that's my sweet spot, you should look out the window."

I don't lift my lips from her skin. "I'm busy."

She laughs, and the sound goes straight to my groin.

"Really," she says. "You definitely don't get to see this in L.A."

I glance out the window, and sure enough, there's a show I've never seen before. "Is that the northern lights?"

She nods. "They're green tonight. Sometimes, they're orange or red. Blue."

"I see a little red on the side over there."

"Oh, yeah." She's whispering now, watching the show outside. "This is why I built these here. There's so much to see. Wildlife and northern lights are just the beginning."

"Amazing," I agree, but now I'm looking down at her. Have I ever been so captivated with a woman? Pulled in so tight that I don't ever want to let go?

"I'm getting warm," she says as she shimmies out of her leggings, then throws them over the side of the turret to the bedroom below.

"Well, by all means, take it all off." I grin and lay back to enjoy a whole new show. Jenna sits and pulls her shirt over her head, then also tosses it aside. "No underwear?"

"Nope." She lies back down and snuggles

against me, pressing her breasts to my still covered torso. The fact that she does all of this with complete confidence and reckless abandon only makes me want her more. "That's better."

"Except, I'm overdressed."

"You're definitely overdressed," she agrees. "You should just take it off. It's nice. You'll see."

I can hear the smile in her voice as I drag my hand from her ass to her neck, then back again.

She has the softest damn skin and smells like citrus.

I hurry out of my clothes, then join her under the covers.

"See?"

"Oh, yeah, it's good." I pull her to me once more and kiss her gently. "You smell amazing."

"Thanks."

She hitches up her leg around my hip, opening herself to me beautifully.

I can't see much of her, only shadows in the darkness, but she feels like heaven.

"If you don't want this to happen," I warn her, "I need you to say something now, sweetheart. Because I'm finding it very hard to hold myself back."

She grins against my mouth. "I'm not telling you to stop, Christian. But I am going to need you to breathe. You're holding your breath."

That's all I need.

I smile and take that breath. I wasn't even aware that I was holding it.

I roll her under me and feast on her lips, my hands gliding over her body. I'm cradled between her legs, my hard, pulsing cock resting against the wetness of her core, and I'm slipping back and forth.

The heat is so fucking inviting, my teeth ache with it.

Before I slip inside her, I need to taste her, so I kiss slowly down her collarbones, then spend some time licking and teasing her nipples.

They pucker beautifully as she arches her back, moaning quietly.

"So amazing," I whisper against her skin, leaving wet kisses down her belly until I finally reach her pussy.

"Fucking hell, you're wet."

"Kind of turned on," she says, lifting her hips in invitation. I cup her ass in my hands and circle her clit with the tip of my nose, then barely graze over it with my tongue. "Oh, God, don't tease me."

"Harder?"

"Much harder."

I wrap my lips around her clit and suck. That's all it takes to make her legs start to shake and her head thrash from side to side.

I press two fingers into her, and my own hips begin to rock against the bed. I can't help it, I'm so fucking turned on right now, at the taste of her, the noises she makes.

I kiss my way back up her body, never moving my hand from her core as I continue to pet her there, softly and then more aggressively.

Her breath is ragged, and she's covered in a light sheen of sweat.

"Need you," I whisper against her neck. She plunges her hands into my hair and kisses my cheek.

"I'm right here."

CHAPTER SIX

Jenna

HOLY FUCKING HELL, the man is good with his hands. And his mouth.

And all the things.

If he were to stop touching me now, I might kill him.

His hair is soft in my fingers, and he smells musky and masculine. And for right now, tonight, under the stars and northern lights, he's all mine.

How did Christian Wolfe come to be here, wrapped around *me*?

"You're overthinking," he whispers into my ear. "And if you're thinking at all, that means I'm not doing my job."

"Oh, you're doing it," I reply and tilt my pelvis up, feeling his hard cock rub against my core.

He growls, then reaches between us, protects us, and presses the tip against my lips.

"Jesus, you're wet."

"Your fault."

"I'll take the blame." And then he pushes inside me until he's balls-deep and pauses. "Fuck."

"So full." I arch my back, and he buries his face in the crook of my neck, licking and nibbling. My entire body is on fire.

I scratch my nails up and down his back as he starts to pick up speed, pushing and pulling in the most intense rhythm. He moves effortlessly, in the sexiest dance I've ever seen.

"You're so damn sexy," he says before kissing me and biting my lower lip. He pushes one hand under my ass, encouraging my hips up, and the slight change in the angle makes my eyes cross.

"Fuuuuck," I moan, just as the first tremors work their way through my body. I'm contracting around him, my entire body tense and on high alert.

"Go over." His voice is firm. It's not a request.

And I can't hold back.

I cry out as my body explodes into light that could rival the night sky above us. Christian's body tenses above me, and he groans as he follows me into his own orgasm.

We're covered in sweat. We're panting.

I'm not sure that I still have arms and legs.

No wait, there they are.

I giggle as I brush my fingertips down his back.

"It's not a good sign when a woman laughs at you after some of the best sex of your life," he says as he boosts himself up on an elbow to stare down at me.

"I'm not laughing at you." I kiss his arm. "I might be delirious."

"Are you okay? Do you need anything?"

I cup his cheek, delighted with the rough whiskers that cover his skin. "I'm perfectly great, and I don't need anything at all."

"Are you tired?" he asks. He shuffles in the bed, then rolls back to me and pulls me into his arms, cradling me so I can rest my head on his chest and listen to his heartbeat.

"Definitely tired." A yawn escapes, the kind that fills your whole chest, and when it works its way out, you have to smack your lips together.

"That sounded like the best yawn ever," Christian says with a laugh, and then succumbs to his own yawn. "That was your fault."

"They're contagious," I agree. "You know what just occurred to me?"

"My physical prowess?"

"Besides that."

He chuckles and kisses my head. "What's that?"

"My tree houses are called Snow Wolf Cottages. And your last name is Wolfe. Is that your real name?"

"No. It's Wagner. My parents gave me a pseud-onym when I was small and first starting in the business."

"Well, I like it," I reply. "But Wagner isn't bad either. Is Wagner still your legal name?"

He pauses, and I feel like I've overstepped a line. But on the other hand, the man was just inside me, and I feel like I can ask whatever I want.

"No, it's Wolfe. It's just easier. I changed it a few years ago."

"Hmm. Well, my real name is Jenna Maxine Hull. And I don't plan to change it."

"Even if you get married?"

I frown, staring out the window at the lights moving across the sky.

"I don't know. I have a lot of business holdings in my name, and I think it would be a pain in the ass to change it all."

"It is a pain," he says and kisses my head again. The man is very affectionate; I'll give him that.

"I guess I'll deal with that if and when it happens." I yawn again and snuggle closer to him. "You're quite comfortable despite being so muscular."

"Thanks. I think."

"It's a compliment."

I can't keep my eyes open now, and the warmth of his arms, with the beating of his heart, is lulling me to sleep.

"Goodnight, Christian."

"Goodnight, beautiful."

***

It's early. The sun hasn't come up yet, but given the time of year, that doesn't mean too much. Being this far north means that we have short days in the winter.

I roll over to look out the windows and can just barely see the first signs of daylight eking their way over the mountain.

It's probably around seven.

I slept like the dead.

Because it's still dark outside, I can't see well in the turret, so I flip the switch for the ceiling stars to help guide my way to the ladder.

I need coffee, STAT.

Careful not to wake Christian, who is still sleeping like a baby, I move around him and down the ladder, then pad downstairs to the kitchen.

While the coffee maker does its thing with the first cup of caffeine, I use the restroom and dig in my overnight bag for the oversized T-shirt I brought to sleep in.

Doesn't look like I'll be doing much sleeping in it.

I smirk as I pull it over my head and return to the kitchen to finish our coffees, then climb the steps, wondering how I'm going to climb that ladder with two full cups of coffee.

But that worry disappears when I reach the top of the stairs and find Christian sitting on the king bed in the loft, looking at his cell phone.

"Good morning."

He looks up, and his eyes warm as he takes me in from head to toe.

"Good morning," he says and accepts the cup I pass him.

"I don't know how you take your coffee, so I just made it the way I take it."

He takes a sip and then smiles. "Sugary."

"Oh, yeah."

He reads the mug. *Blow me I'm hot.*

"I mean, you *are* hot."

He laughs and sets his coffee aside. "Let me see yours."

I oblige him.

I do my own stunts.

"I even climb ladders," I confirm and earn a laugh from the sexiest man I think I've ever seen.

Ever.

Before I can take another sip, he takes my mug and sets it next to his, then tumbles me back onto the bed.

"We're awake too early," he says and pulls me against him.

"Don't you have to go ski?"

"Nope." He grins. "Everyone needs a day off now and again. Let's go get breakfast. It's early enough to beat the crowds."

I think it over, juggling my day. "I have to go to town anyway to check on the house."

"And you have to eat," he reminds me.

"Yes. I'm feeling particularly hungry this morning."

"You burned quite a few calories last night." He shifts, tucking me under him and pinning my hands over my head. He's stretched out above me, and his body is long and lean in the early morning light just beginning to come through the windows.

"Are we about to burn a few more?"

His lips twitch as he nestles his way between my legs. I'm already turned on.

I'm permanently aroused when I'm with him.

My hands are suddenly free as he dives for the bedside table and returns with a condom. Once he's taken care of that little detail, he covers me once more, but I'm able to touch him now, and I can't keep my hands off of him.

"I could become addicted to you," he says as he slips inside me and immediately begins to move in a steady, quick rhythm. "The sounds you make, the way you grip my dick like a damn vise."

I press on his shoulder, and he lets me flip us over so I can ride him, bracing my hands on his chest.

He grips my hips, his fingertips biting into my ass. It's fucking delicious.

I ride us both into a frenzy, and just as we both come, he sits up, wraps his arms around me, and kisses me like his life depends on it.

It's the most intense sex I've ever had in my life.

Finally, when we're able to talk, he says, "I'm so hungry."

I grin. "Let's get ready and go get some food."

"Excellent plan."

***

"It looks like the guys did a good job," I say an hour later as we walk through my house. "The water's gone, and they said they replaced the pipe."

"Is there damage?" he asks.

"Yeah, I have some drywall to replace, and I've got my fingers crossed that the floor will be okay once it dries. It's original to the house, so I'd like to keep it if at all possible."

"I really like your house," he says as he walks around the kitchen.

"I'm sure it's much smaller than what you're used to."

"It's smaller, but it's beautiful." He shrugs. "I'm only one person. Why do I need a twelve-thousand-square-foot house?"

"Your house is *twelve-thousand square feet*?

Jesus, this one is eighteen hundred."

"It's pretty ridiculous," he says with a nod. "But I have to invest somewhere, and real estate is usually a sure bet."

"Very true, and exactly why I started this business. I had some inheritance and wanted to do something that would make me money. Real estate in Cunningham Falls is expensive, and only on the rise because of the number of celebrities we have here. It's quickly becoming another Vail or Breckenridge."

"Really?" He leans on the countertop and crosses his arms over his chest.

"Oh, yeah. We have a few locals who went on to be celebrities. Joslyn Meyers is one."

"I've met her," he says with a nod. "She seems nice."

"She was a little younger than me, but I know her family. She's very sweet and super successful. Oh, and the football player Tucker McCloud is from here."

"So, Cunningham Falls is no stranger to the rich and famous."

"No." I smile. "We're tucked away and still off the map enough that many celebrities like to come here for vacation."

"I can see that. It's one of the reasons that Nina chose this resort for me." He glances over my shoulder and smiles. "I have to know what's up with the funny mugs."

"It's a joke." I turn to look at all of my mugs sitting in the glass cabinet. "People give them to me all the time. I've never been a morning person, and I have to say, these mugs make me smile and less grouchy in the morning. But I've accumulated so many, I can't keep them all here, so I started stocking them in my rentals."

"They are funny." He reaches out and tucks a piece of my hair behind my ear. "Should we go eat?"

"Absolutely." I lock up my house, and we drive less than a mile to downtown and my favorite breakfast spot, Ed's Diner. It's been in town since way before I was born, and the original owner, Ed himself, is still alive and well and manning the grill.

We're shown to a table, but Christian is spotted right away by what I'm assuming are tourists. They whisper amongst themselves, watching as we sit, and then whip out their phones to take photos from several tables away.

"And it begins," Christian mutters. His whole demeanor changes from relaxed to on guard. His muscles tense. His eyes go hard.

"Hi," a woman who has come to stand at our table says. "Can I please get a photo with you?"

Christian looks at me, then stands and gives her a fake smile. "Sure."

And that's all it takes for a line to form.

"Oh my God, Jenna, I didn't know that you're friends with Christian Wolfe," Misty Maddox says as I pull myself out of the booth. I can't stand that bitch. She's nosy and a mean girl in the classic sense of the term.

I ignore her and walk into the kitchen. Ed looks up in surprise.

"Hey there, baby girl," he says with a wide smile. "I love it when a pretty girl walks into my kitchen."

"Hey, Ed. I need a favor."

"Anything."

I explain the situation to him while trying to keep an eye on what's happening in the dining room.

"I'm sorry to disrupt the diner like this. I didn't expect it. This town is used to having celebrities walking about."

"The tourists aren't," he says with a scowl. "I'll get some food ready to go for you so you can get out of here. I'm working on it right now. Do you know what you want?"

We didn't get that far.

"Honestly, whatever is easiest is great. Neither of us is picky."

"Didn't get a chance to look at the menu?" He winks at me and turns to the grill. "I've got this. Go rescue him."

I lean in and kiss Ed's cheek and hurry back out to the dining room. The crowd around him has grown, but his smile hasn't slipped.

He looks cool and completely at ease.

But I can see the tension in his muscles.

"I just think you're the best actor in Hollywood today," Misty says as she sidles up next to him, sure to press her fake boobs against his side. "I've seen *every single movie* you've made."

"Well, I appreciate that," he says and smiles for the camera, then brushes her aside so he can give the next person his attention.

"Sorry, guys," I announce as I push my way back to him. "We have to leave."

"But you just got here," someone yells from the back.

"This isn't a photo op. The man is on vacation," I reply just as Ed muscles his way through the crowd with a bag full of hot food.

"Here you go," he says kindly. "There's plenty there since I didn't know what you might want."

"Appreciate it," Christian says with a nod. "How much do we owe you?"

"I think *I* owe you this much, after the way these idiots behaved."

He doesn't even try to lower his voice, and it makes me smile. Ed always did call it like he saw it.

"Thanks again," I say and link my fingers with Christian's, but he pulls away, not even sparing me a glance.

That hurts, I'm not going to lie.

But I shouldn't assume that just because we're doing the deed that we're a couple.

Because we aren't.

And I need to remember that.

"Follow me," I say to Christian and walk out the door to my car. I set the food in the backseat, and once Christian is next to me, I take off. Most of the people in the diner are watching us pull away. "I'm really sorry about that."

"I should have known," he says with a sigh and rubs his fingertips over his forehead. "I just wasn't prepared for it."

"I've never seen anything like that here in town."

He shrugs a shoulder. "Look, I need to explain something to you. I let go of your hand—"

"I know, it was dumb of me to try and hold your hand. I'm sorry. We're totally *not* a couple, and I shouldn't have done that."

"Stop talking," he says, surprising me. "That's not what I was going to say. You can hold my hand all you want, Jenna. But not in public. Jesus, this is fucked-up." He rubs his forehead again. "Someone will take a photo, and it'll go viral. According to the press, I'm still dating Serena, which is a lie and it's ridiculous, but it is what it is."

"I forget that you're not just a guy," I admit softly as I turn onto the road that leads up to the tree house. "Because you *are* that with me, and I don't mean that as an insult. You're a great guy, and you're special to *me*."

"I get it," he says. "We know each other outside of all the drama, and it's the most normal relationship I have. I'm enjoying the hell out of it."

"And then I take you to a diner where you're accosted."

He laughs now, and I can see his body start to relax. "Well, it was my fault. I let my guard down, and I can't do that, especially in public."

"That must be exhausting."

I glance over at him. He's watching the road ahead.

"It can be."

"Well, Ed hooked us up with a ton of food, so at least we still get to eat breakfast."

"That's the important thing." He takes my hand and kisses my knuckles. "I'm sorry that I pulled away. I saw the hurt in your eyes when I did it, and I wanted to pull you to me and kiss the fuck out of you."

"And here I thought I had a poker face."

"No." He kisses my hand again. "I read people for a living. You may think you're hiding your feelings, but they're all there in your eyes, fancy face."

"Did you just call me *fancy face*?"

He nods. "You're stunning, Jenna. Someone's told you that before."

I shrug. "Yeah. I hear that I look like Grace

Kelly a lot."

"You're more beautiful than Grace Kelly."

"It's just the luck of the draw," I reply as I pull into my parking space and cut the engine. Neither of us moves to leave the car. "It's genetics. And while I'm grateful that my mom and dad had the right combination of DNA to produce pretty babies, I'd like to think that I'm also smart and funny and kind. Because those are the things that matter at the end of the day."

"You *are* those things, Jenna. And trust me when I say that I've met my share of beautiful people. You're right, it's the other things that matter, and it's too often that what someone's face looks like is the priority. Especially in my world."

"You have a pretty face," I reply and give his cheek a little slap. "So pretty."

"You like to be spanked, don't you?"

I laugh now and reach back for our food. "I'm sassy when I'm hungry."

"No, I think you're just sassy. And I'm going to keep calling you fancy face."

"Can I call you pretty boy?"

"No. Absolutely not."

CHAPTER SEVEN

Jenna

"**A**RE YOU HERE?" Grace calls from my front door. I'm in town for the day, trying to get everything figured out with my house after the surprise water damage the other day.

"Back here!" I call out and finish putting away the mess that the repairmen made.

"Hey, friend," she says when she finds me. Grace is short and curvy with curly red hair and the sweetest face ever made. She just might be the sweetest *person* ever made.

"Hi," I reply and pull her in for a hug. "I'm excited I get to see you today."

"Same. We have a lot to talk about. You've been holding out on me."

I bite my lip and look away, but she's right. I've totally been holding out on her.

"Not to mention," she continues, "I appreciate

the ride up to the Lodge. It'll be fun to see Jacob in his element."

"It's my pleasure." I reach for my coat and hat and lead her out to the garage. When we're on our way, Grace doesn't waste any time.

"Christian Wolfe."

Just the mention of his name sends shivers over my skin.

"Yes?"

"Oh, please, I know he's staying at your place, and I also know that you were seen with him downtown yesterday at Ed's."

"The people in this town talk too much," I grumble as we head up the mountain road. "First of all, I should have told you myself."

"Damn right," she mutters.

"And I'm sorry that you didn't hear it from me. Just please tell me you didn't hear it from Misty."

"Jesus, no," she says as if I just asked her if she'd like to take a bath in split pea soup. "I don't talk to that bitch."

"I thought maybe you ran into her," I reply with a sigh. "So, yes, Christian has been staying in the tree house for a few days now."

"And you're hanging out with him."

I glance over at her, and she looks like an excited teenager, which only makes me giggle.

"You could call it that."

"SHUT THE FUCK UP!" She slaps my arm and then squeals in the seat. "Are you sleeping with him? Jenna Maxine, you better tell me if you're sleeping with him."

"You're going to make a great mom, what with using the middle name and all."

"Spill it!"

"We do sleep sometimes, yes."

"I can't believe it," she says, shaking her head and making her curls bounce. "One of my best friends is fucking Christian Wolfe, the man I've daydreamed about for *years*."

"You *are* happily married to the sexiest Brit I know," I remind her.

"Oh, trust me, Jacob is damn hot and rocks my world pretty much every day. No complaints there at all. But *Christian Wolfe*."

"Yeah, he's sexy."

"I can't even," she says and sighs as I pull into the valet at the Lodge. "Before we get out, I just have to know. Is it as good as I think it is?"

I smile and cock a brow. "Girl, I didn't know it could be this good."

"Damn it, I knew it."

A young man opens her door, and wraps both arms around her, helping her out of the car and making sure she's safely inside as if she's made of glass.

"That was nice of him," I comment as we walk

into the restaurant.

"Jacob's trained them to be extra careful with me in the snow," she says. "You know how clumsy I am, and with being pregnant, well, he's protective."

"I love it," I reply, and we take a seat near the windows that look out over the ski runs, watching people get on and off the chairlift. "It's busy around here."

"I see much less of Jacob this time of year," she says and takes a sip of her water. "He has plenty of staff and could leave it all up to them, but he's very hands-on."

"And you like that he's hands-on," I reply with a wink, making her laugh.

"Damn right."

Just after we order our lunch, both Jacob and Christian come walking into the dining room, smiling at us.

"Holy shit, they could burn this place down with those smiles," I whisper.

"It should be illegal for them to be in the same place at the same time," she agrees and stands so she can kiss her husband, who sweeps her up into his arms and kisses her as if no one is watching.

It's damn adorable.

"Hey, fancy face," Christian says and leans in to kiss my cheek, but he's careful not to touch me otherwise and glances around to see if anyone is watching or aiming their phone at us.

I don't like that he has to live his life like this. And that I, in turn, have to do the same. We haven't defined our relationship, but I'd say we're a couple, and I am not the kind of person who hides things that matter.

And this matters.

"Darling, I'd like to introduce you to Christian Wolfe," Jacob says and steps back when Grace turns to greet Christian.

But in true Grace fashion, she trips on the chair and ends up in Christian's arms.

"Oops," she says as her face brightens.

"Pleased to meet you," Christian says with a laugh as he helps her back to her feet.

"I've pictured meeting you many ways over the years," she says, "but knocked-up and swollen was never one of them."

"No?" Christian's eyebrows climb into his hairline, and his eyes are full of humor. "How did it go?"

"Well, I *did* end up in your arms, so…nailed it." She laughs and leans into Jacob when he wraps an arm around her. "And we'll just leave the rest to your imagination. I'm a fan, though, so it's really great to meet you."

"Grace is one of my dearest friends," I inform him as they all take seats around the table.

"And how did the two of you meet?" Christian

asks them.

"I fell into his arms, too," Grace says. "But, I'm always falling, so that's nothing new. Have you guys eaten?"

"I'm starving," Christian says and accepts a menu from the waitress. "I'd love a burger and fries, ranch on the side, please."

"I wish I could eat like that," Grace says and rubs her belly. "I'm not active enough these days."

"You're eating for two," I remind her with a laugh. "You could get away with a burger now and then."

"I'll stick with the salad I ordered," she replies, and Jacob laughs.

"She'll send me out for a burger for dinner, don't let her fool you."

"I totally will," she says with a nod. "So, Christian, are you enjoying Cunningham Falls?"

"So far," he says with a nod. "I came up to learn to ski for a movie, and it's been really fun. The town is beautiful, and I have a stunning tour guide, as well, so I can't complain."

The compliment sends my heart beating a mile a minute. He's sweet, and although he's not super affectionate in public—for good reason—he's very attentive and charming, and the man can't keep his hands off me when we're in private.

Let's be honest, I can't complain either.

Lunch is fun, and just when Jacob and Grace

have said goodbye, and Christian and I are heading out, I get a text from Max.

Where are you? I'm at the tree house.

I hurry and call him, rolling my eyes.

"Everything okay?" Christian asks.

"Yeah, it's my brother."

"Yello," Max answers, sounding happy-go-lucky. "Where are you?"

"I'm on my way there, but don't go in any of the units. They're all rented out."

"Oh, cool. Good for you. Are you almost here?"

"Yeah, I'll be there in five minutes. See you soon." I hang up as the valet brings my car around. "Can I give you a ride, Mr. Wolfe?"

"Sure." We get inside, and I drive off toward the tree houses. "Why did you drive down?"

"I was actually in town and picked up Grace there," I reply. "I didn't know Max was back in town."

We pull up next to my brother's SUV and climb out. It's snowing like crazy, and the wind has started to pick up.

"Hey," I say and hug Max. "Let's go in, the weather is getting nuts."

"I thought you said they're rented?" he asks, eyeing Christian.

"They are, but this is Christian. He's renting the Tamarack. I've been staying with him."

I ignore Max's scowl and walk into the tree house. Christian sheds his ski gear in the entryway while Max follows me into the kitchen.

"Are you guys in here?" I hear Brad ask from the doorway. "Oh, hey, Christian."

"Hi, Brad. Jenna and Max are inside."

"Are you going to tell me what's going on?" Max demands, shooting daggers at me from his position on the other side of the kitchen island.

"A pipe burst at my house," I reply and set to work making myself a cup of decaf. "Want some coffee?"

"No, I don't want any fucking coffee. I want to know what in the hell is going on."

I turn to my brother and prop my hands on my hips. "You don't get to talk to me like that."

"Why are you staying with a guest? My house is empty. Hell, Brad has an extra bedroom."

Christian walks into the room and smiles at Max. "We haven't met. I'm Christian Wolfe. I've heard a lot about you."

Max looks at Christian's outstretched hand and then glares at me without accepting it.

"You're fucking around with a guest?"

"Oh, Jesus, Max. Calm the hell down."

"I'm gone for a week, and all hell breaks loose."

I can't help the snort-laugh that comes out of me. "You're being really dramatic. All hell has not broken loose unless you count the fact that my house got flooded. Then, yes, that was hell."

"And you're screwing around—"

"So, here's the thing," Christian says calmly, but his voice, and his eyes are hard. "I get that you don't know me from Adam and that it's a surprise to you that she's staying here with me, but Jenna isn't a child."

"She's my *sister*," Max replies, then pins Brad with a stare. "Did you know about this?"

"She *is* a grown woman, man. And I like him." Brad shrugs, and Max's jaw drops.

"Why are you so weird about this?" I demand as I put sugar and cream into my coffee. "I hate to break the news to you, but I wasn't a virgin when I met Christian."

All three men scowl, and I can't help but let out another laugh.

"It seems unethical to sleep with a client," Max says, his jaw firm.

"Or you just want to meddle in my life, the way you always do. But I have news for you, Max, I'm fine. I don't need you to meddle in my life any more than you want that from me. Because, trust me when I say, I know who you should marry, should've married *years* ago. I saw her just the other day, and she's everything you need in your life. But you're a pain in the ass."

"This isn't about me and Willa," Max says.

"See? You even know who I'm talking about!"

"Jenna—" Christian begins, but Brad interrupts him.

"Leave them be," Brad says, "they do this all the time, and they'll be back to being friends in about ten minutes."

"I don't need you to always protect me," I continue. "I know you think you need to, but you don't, Max. I'm a smart woman, I have my shit together, and if I want to fuck every guest who walks in here, I will."

"No," Christian says, his eyes full of lust and anger, "you won't."

"Oh, Lord." I hang my head and scratch my cheek. "I'm surrounded by alpha men."

"Jenna," Max begins, his voice calmer now, "I left town a week ago. *He* wasn't here, and you weren't sleeping with anyone. And now he's here, you're shacked up with him, and I had no idea."

"I don't need to ask your permission," I remind him. "And we're not *shacked up*. I'm staying here until my place is fixed and dry, which should be in another day or so."

"Still could have stayed at my place," he says but then glances over at Christian. "I know who you are. And believe me when I say, I don't care. If you fuck up with her, I'll bust that pretty face of yours."

"I do *not* have a pretty face," Christian says, looking about in exasperation. "Why do you and your sister keep saying that?"

"I'm not kidding," Max replies. "If you hurt her, I'll hurt you."

"For fuck's sake," I mutter and turn to Brad. "Why did you guys come, and can you please get him out of here?"

"I just wanted to say hi, and Brad was in the neighborhood."

"Well, hi." I sip my coffee and stare him down. "I should probably get back to work. Don't you have an empire to run?"

"You're always more important," Max replies and pulls me in for a tight hug. "And I think you're the bee's knees."

"I think you're the cat's meow," I say begrudgingly. "A meddling cat."

"Hey, it's what I do." He pulls back and grins, then steals my cup and takes a sip. "God, how can you drink this so sweet?"

"Get out," I reply, shooing both brothers out the door. "I'm glad you're home, now go away. Call Willa. Take her out on a date."

"Willa doesn't want to see me," Max replies and offers me a sad smile before leaving. "And stop trying to make that happen."

"Love you."

I shut the door and turn to Christian. "Sorry about that."

"You give him too much shit," he says and

crosses his arms over his chest.

"Why?"

"Because he's your brother, and he just wants the best for you."

"Not you, too." I roll my eyes and move to walk past him, but he catches my arm, keeping me next to him.

"Why do you have issues with being protected?"

"I don't," I reply. "I understand family looking out for family. My father was the police chief of Cunningham Falls before Brad. Protection is what my family does.

"But, sometimes, Max goes overboard with it. He was flat out rude to you, and there's no need for that. I'm pushing thirty for godsake, Christian. I do have it together, and I can sleep with whomever I please, as long as it isn't hurting anyone else. My brothers have a tendency to see me as weak. They won't admit it, but it's because I'm a woman, and let me tell you, I've had it up to my waxed eyebrows with being placated for my gender. I have to fight contractors, sub-contractors, and everyone else you can think of in my job to be respected as a businessperson."

"They're not contractors," he says. "They're family."

"Exactly. They should know better." I pull away and walk a few feet into the living room then turn back to him. "Why are we arguing about this?"

"I just think it's nice that you have family that looks out for you. Sometimes, we take it for granted, and I'm pointing that out to you."

I take a deep breath. "Max makes me crazy."

Christian's lips twitch. "He's your brother. That's his job."

"He excels at it. Always has. We're pretty close in age."

Christian's phone rings, and he pulls it out of his pocket, still looking at me. He doesn't check the caller id when he answers.

"This is Wolfe."

He smiles and holds his hand out to me, and I immediately take it. He spins me once, then pulls me into his arms and hugs me.

"How's it going, Luke? Yeah, things are good here. It's an awesome resort."

He's chatting with his friend and slowly dancing me around the floor, making me giggle into his chest.

His very hard chest.

"Let me ask her, just a sec." He pulls the phone down on his chin. "Do you have room for Luke and his wife next week? They're flexible on dates."

"Here in the tree houses?"

Christian nods, and I mentally check the calendar. "I do have room in the Spruce unit Wednesday through Saturday."

"Did you hear that?" he asks into the phone. "Great, I'll have her pencil you in. See you soon."

He hangs up, tosses his phone on the counter, and immediately dances me around the room, faster than I'm comfortable with, but he's excellent. Poised. So damn charming.

"Who am I penciling in?" I ask, my breath coming faster.

"Luke Williams and his wife."

I trip over my own feet. "Luke Williams the movie star?"

Christian laughs. "I hate to break this to you, but you're dancing with a movie star right now."

I blink quickly and try to gather myself. Grace always had a crush on Christian, but Luke was *my* crush, and he's going to be here on Wednesday.

In my place.

"Are you going to be okay?" Christian asks. "Also, I should add that this isn't great for my self-esteem."

I laugh and push up on my toes to kiss him. "I'm going to be great, and I don't think of you as a big-time movie star."

"No? How do you think of me?"

His blue eyes are doing that smolder thing again as he effortlessly moves me around the room.

I'm falling in love with him.

I swallow hard and smile up at him.

"You're Christian, a sexy man who's come into my life and made it exciting. Sexy."

He leans down to press his forehead to mine.

"Safe," I add as he moves in for the kiss of a lifetime.

"We're both safe here."

CHAPTER EIGHT

Christian

"**G**ETTING HERE ISN'T EASY," Luke says the following Wednesday as he and his wife, Natalie, climb out of their rented SUV. They're both smiling and looking around, taking it all in. "But it's fucking beautiful here."

"Worth the trip for sure," Natalie says and walks over to me. Jenna is standing next to me, unable to speak.

It's actually kind of cute.

"I'm Natalie Williams," she says with a smile, holding out her hand for mine. "And I've heard so many great things about you from Luke."

"Christian Wolfe," I reply with a smile and then introduce the woman I've become way too used to having next to me. "This is Jenna Hull, the owner of Snow Wolf Cottages where I've been staying. Jenna, this is Luke and Natalie Williams."

"Hi," Jenna says and shakes their hands. "It's cold out here this afternoon. Let's get you both inside and settled."

She glances up at me, the nerves still apparent in her expressive blue eyes, but her body language is confident as she leads us all into the middle tree house.

"This is absolutely amazing," Natalie says and pulls out her camera from her oversized handbag. "I hope you don't mind me taking photos. I'm a photographer, and this is just screaming at my inner artist."

"Of course, not," Jenna says with a smile. "I'm so happy that you like it. But wait until you see the best part."

I wait downstairs as she leads them both upstairs.

"Look at that turret!" Natalie exclaims. I can hear the shutter on her camera clicking. "Jenna, I'll be happy to send you copies of my photos, if you like."

"I would love that," Jenna replies as they come back downstairs. "So, that's the whole place. It's not huge, but it's cozy."

"It's perfect," Luke assures her. "We appreciate you squeezing us in."

"It's my pleasure," she says. "You'll be able to watch the skiers during the day, as that's one of the ski runs. At night, the whole place is lit up, and you can see the lights in town from the village."

"I love how everything is decorated for Christmas," Natalie says, and I'm immediately reminded that I'll be leaving in just a couple of weeks. I'm scheduled to fly out on the 23rd so I can spend the holidays with my family before I start filming Luke's project.

Time is moving too damn fast.

"Is there anything specific you'd like to do while you're here that I can help with?" Jenna asks.

"Yes," Natalie immediately replies. "I'm going to need a spa, and I think it would be fun to have dinner one night with you and Christian and any of your close friends."

Jenna's eyes immediately find mine in surprise.

"Don't worry," Natalie says, reaching out to hold Jenna's hand. "Christian didn't say anything, but I can see by the way you look at each other that you've got something going on. I think it's awesome."

"We came to see the resort, the town, and to spend some time with Christian," Luke adds, and I can only sit back and watch the interaction with fascination. Jenna is taking it all in stride as if they're just a normal couple of guests, and a part of me that I didn't even know was anxious lets go.

"I can certainly arrange for a spa day for you, Natalie. And I'm quite sure we can pull together a dinner on Friday." She looks at me for confirmation, and I nod, smiling at her.

Jesus, she's beautiful. Smart.

And kind.

Luke wraps his arm around his wife's shoulders and buries his lips in her hair. Whatever he says makes her blush.

Natalie is a beautiful woman. With long, dark hair and green eyes, she's quite stunning. And right now, she's looking at Luke as if he hung the moon.

"Get him away from the kids for a bit, and he can't keep his hands off me," she says with a laugh.

"How many kids do you have?" Jenna asks.

"Four," Luke replies, and Jenna's eyes widen in surprise.

"Sounds like he can't keep his hands off of you when the kids are around, either," Jenna says with a laugh. "I love that. My parents were the same way. There are three of us, and they never had any qualms about being affectionate with each other around us."

"Our kids won't be strangers to affection," Luke agrees. "Christian, when can you and I meet to talk business?"

"I have a ski lesson tomorrow morning, and then I'm free," I reply. "Would you like to join me for the lesson?"

"I'd love to," he says immediately, his face lighting up in anticipation. "I ski quite well, actually."

"Oh, great," Natalie says, her voice dry. "Please don't break anything."

"You need to have more faith in me, baby," he says, and Natalie simply laughs.

"I have all the faith in the world, but I don't need my husband to break an arm. I need you."

"I think that's our cue to leave," Jenna says with a laugh. "If you need anything, my cell number is in the book on the table, along with the Wi-Fi info."

"Thank you, Jenna," Natalie says. "This is truly a treat."

"Enjoy your time away from the kiddos," Jenna says with a wink and leads me out of the unit and over to the Tamarack. "They're nice."

"Agreed."

"You haven't said much." She leans on the kitchen counter, watching me with happy, blue eyes. I love how expressive her eyes are. I slowly walk to her and cage her in, leaning on the counter with my arms on either side of her. My lips are inches from hers. "What are you thinking?"

That I don't ever want to leave Cunningham Falls. That I've come to life since I've known you, and I don't care how crazy that sounds.

"That you're pretty great."

She smiles and drags her fingertips down my cheek. "I like your whiskers."

"I'm usually clean-shaven."

She shrugs. "I like that, too. You are a handsome man, Christian." She frowns as if she regrets what she just said.

"What's wrong?"

"I sometimes worry that when I say things like *you're handsome* or *you're talented* that you'll get the wrong idea and think that I'm doing this with you because of your career. Because of your celebrity status."

"I don't think that," I reply immediately, at once relieved and humbled because I can see that it's completely true. She couldn't care less about the celebrity side of me, and I didn't think that was something I'd ever find. I lean in closer. "I know you're doing *this* with me because you're hot for my body."

She giggles and then lets loose with a full belly laugh and leans in to my chest.

"I mean," she says when she finally catches her breath, "that's true. Your body is stellar. Like, it's something to write home about."

"I work out," I reply as if it's no big deal, enjoying the fun banter.

"Hmm, I can tell." Her eyes and hands move over my torso, and my skin is suddenly on fire everywhere she touches. "Have I mentioned that I'm a fan of your arms?"

"I don't think so."

"You should take this shirt off so I can see them better." She blinks up at me coyly and bites her lip, and I know in this moment I'd do pretty much anything she asked.

She's a fucking siren.

I whip my shirt over my head and let it fall to the floor, and Jenna's fingertips immediately trace the muscles in my arms.

"Seriously, these should come with a warning label."

"What would it say?"

"May cause panties to combust," she replies, and it's my turn to laugh now. Her fingers trail down my stomach to the waistband of my jeans. She pokes her finger inside, running along the edge of my jeans and against my skin, and every nerve ending on my body sizzles.

I want to turn her around and fuck her against the countertop, but I hold back, wanting to see how far she'll take this foreplay of hers.

And let's be real, it feels fucking amazing.

I'm rewarded for my patience when she drops through my arms and down into a squat, and unfastens my pants, unleashing my pulsing hard cock.

I bury my hands in her hair, but she pulls away and raises a brow as she looks up at me. "Keep your hands on the countertop," she says.

My cock dances in anticipation.

It seems Jenna wants to play the boss right now, and I'm in no position to fight her on it.

My knuckles are white on the countertop's edge as she takes me in her palm, then runs that little, pink tongue from my balls to the tip and back again. It's the most erotic thing I've ever seen, her gorgeous face sucking me in and making my damn eyes cross.

My jeans are still hitched around my ass, and I reach back to grab a condom from my pocket and flick it onto the counter, then grab onto the granite again as she milks me, licking and pulling with her mouth, her hands, and sending me straight into the only heaven I'll ever know.

"Jenna, I don't want to come in your mouth."

She ignores me, on a mission to make me lose it, but I grab her shoulders and pull her up, kiss her hard, then turn her around and bend her over the island, one hand planted in the middle of her back and the other working her pants down.

"I wasn't done," she says with a pout. I lean over and press my lips to her ear.

"You only get to be the boss for so long, fancy face." I protect us both and then push inside her, reveling at how wet she is, how fucking *ready* she is. "You make me crazy. I want you so badly I can't see straight."

It isn't soft or gentle or slow. It's hard and fast, and over almost as quickly as it began, but I'm no less spent.

She undoes me. I've never lost myself with anyone before. I always know exactly what I'm doing with the woman I'm with.

But everything with Jenna is different.

"Wow," she whispers, pushing her hair out of

her face and smiling back at me. "That was fun. I should do that more often."

"You'll kill me." I pull out of her, then tug her into my arms so I can kiss her silly. "I didn't hurt you?"

"You'd never hurt me."

The faith she has in me is astounding.

"Never on purpose."

***

"Do you do your own stunts?" Max asks me a few nights later when we're all having dinner with Luke and Natalie. The girls, and by that I mean Jenna, Natalie, Grace, and Hannah, are chatting in the loft of the biggest tree house where we all gathered this evening.

Jenna had dinner catered by the Italian restaurant in town. I may have gained ten pounds today, and I'll need to work out extra hard tomorrow to work it off, but I don't care.

The food is delicious, and the company is excellent.

"Some of them," I reply and take a sip of wine. I'm with Max, Brad, Jacob, and Luke, and we're sitting in the living area. "Not the ones that require heights."

"I'll do those for you," Jenna calls from up above and blows me a kiss, making me grin. She's had a couple of glasses of wine, and she's fucking adorable.

"Thanks, babe."

She winks and disappears again.

"Will you be comfortable doing most of the skiing in the movie?" Luke asks me. He hasn't had much of anything to drink, but I can tell that he's at ease, enjoying the conversation.

"Definitely. I should have taken it up years ago."

"You're a natural," he agrees. "It was fun joining you during your lessons. Thanks for letting me tag along."

"No, it was fun to have you. I'm glad you approve."

He nods, and we listen with half an ear as the other men begin talking about a new business that's trying to move into town, but how the city council voted it down.

"I like it here," Luke says softly. "Nat and I discussed the idea of buying a place here for vacations. We have a big family, so it would get used."

"That would be cool."

"Jenna's friends are nice."

I nod, not saying too much until Luke finally sighs and leans forward.

"You're stubborn, you know that?"

"I like to think of it as private," I reply with a smile. "Besides, I agree with you. It's awesome here."

"I see what you have here, Christian."

I can't reply. I can only swallow hard and watch my wine swirl around my glass. I don't want to get too comfortable here, no matter how much I love it. "It's temporary."

"Join me outside," Luke says and leads me out onto the balcony. It's snowing, but it's unusually warm. There's no wind.

It's perfectly quiet.

"Does it have to be temporary?"

I turn to him and frown. "What are you talking about? Of course, it does. My life, my career is in L.A. I'm not ready to retire."

"I'm not suggesting that," Luke says with a sigh. "Let me back up. I know I don't know you well, Christian, but I see a huge difference in you since I saw you a few months ago in Seattle. Whatever has happened here in Montana has been good for you."

"I won't deny that." I watch as a deer walks down the ski slope. "But my life isn't here, Luke."

"You can always travel on location. You do most of the time anyway. You live in L.A., but we're filming the movie in Vancouver."

I look at him, wondering where he's going with this.

"There's nothing that says you can't be here, with Jenna, in between films."

"Come on, you know it's not that easy. Between

films are press junkets and appearances. Magazine articles. TV shows. It's never-ending."

He sighs. "Don't let the industry fuck up what you've found here, Christian. Because from where I stand, you've found something that feeds your soul. And if I've learned anything in the amount of time that I've been in this business, it's that it'll suck the life right out of you if you aren't careful."

"How do you do it?" I turn to him and prop my hands on my hips. "You have a beautiful wife, kids, and you live in Seattle. Yet you're still as relevant in Hollywood as you were ten years ago."

"I set boundaries," he says thoughtfully, rubbing his chin. "I left it, not intending to return. It had gutted me. But films are what I'm passionate about, and I eventually learned how to balance it. I don't do press. I'm only on location for a few days. I don't act anymore, so there's that."

"Until I met Jenna, I would have told you that acting was the best part of my life."

"And now?"

I sigh. "I just don't know how I can make it work. But I know that I'm enjoying her, and my time here. I'm honest with her."

"Are you?" He tilts his head to the side. "Are you even honest with yourself? Because the man I saw months ago was miserable, and the man standing before me now is alive."

"Is this why you brought Natalie up here?"

"Partly," he admits. "I wanted to see you skiing, to make sure the role's a good fit. It is."

"Not everyone gets the happily ever after that you got," I remind him.

"They should," he says with a satisfied grin. "Because it's fucking great, kid. It's better than any Oscar sitting on my shelf. I mean, did you *see* her?"

My lips twitch. "I did."

"I would give it all up tomorrow if she asked me to, but here's the kicker: she never would."

Jenna wouldn't either.

"Ah, there it is," he says with a smile. "You get it. Enjoy the last few weeks here in your insulated bubble without press, where you get to be a man with a beautiful woman. But just remember that you don't have to choose one life over the other."

I push my hand through my hair. "Thank you."

"You can name your first kid after me."

I stare at him in horrified surprise, making him laugh.

"I'm kidding. Sort of."

"I need more wine."

CHAPTER NINE

Jenna

"THIS IS SO NICE," Natalie says from the lounge chair next to mine. We're sitting in the tranquil area of the spa at the Lodge, drinking hot tea, wrapped in fluffy, white robes.

"I'm glad you talked me into it." I sip my tea and sigh with happiness. "I don't remember the last time I did something like this."

"You strike me as being a bit of a workaholic," Nat replies. "Not that there's anything wrong with that, as long as you take care of yourself."

She smiles softly. Natalie has an air of absolute calm about her. With four kids and a celebrity husband, I would expect her to be more frantic.

"I lose track of time." I shrug and sip more of my tea. "But maybe I should just have a standing appointment once a month for a massage."

"Atta girl," she says with a nod. "I approve

whole-heartedly. Now, let's get to the good stuff. Tell me about Christian."

I laugh and set my tea aside, then snuggle down in my robe, thinking about the sexiest man alive.

I mean, *People* magazine dubbed him that less than six months ago.

"He's a nice guy."

Nat wrinkles her nose. "I mean, tell me the good stuff. I promise, I'm a vault."

"He's everything I never expected."

"That's more like it." She rubs her hands together and wiggles her eyebrows. "He seems so nice, and Luke has great things to say about him."

"He is nice. And he doesn't have a chip on his shoulder like I thought a super famous guy would have."

"That's a plus because, trust me, there are plenty of those. Not that I've met many. Luke keeps me and the kids separate from the professional stuff as much as he can."

"Really?" I tilt my head, watching her with interest. "How is that possible?"

"Luke had already set a lot of boundaries when I met him," she says, rubbing a finger over her lips as she thinks about it. "He was done with acting by then, and he still refuses to do much press. He's fiercely private. I think the paparazzi give him anxiety, and now that he's not been in front of the camera for years, they pretty much leave him alone.

"I will go to award ceremonies with him, like the Oscars, but we never take the kids with us."

"I think that's awesome," I say quietly. "That he's managed to balance both family and a demanding career."

"It's not easy. If I weren't so laid back, I don't know if it would have worked." She narrows her eyes at me. "You don't seem like a laid-back kind of girl."

"I'm more type-A," I reply with a grin.

"If you're going to make it work with someone like Christian, there will be times that you'll have to just go with the flow. Schedules change, life is interrupted, and it can be inconvenient."

"Go with the flow," I murmur. "That actually makes sense."

"Also, if you're a jealous person, this will not work." She stands to pour herself some more tea.

"I'm not a jealous person, but I'm also not the kind of woman who is okay with being hidden."

Nat raises a brow as she sits back in her chair. "You're hiding?"

I explain how the press thinks that Christian is with Serena for the sake of the movie release, and how careful he is not to touch me in public.

"I'm not okay with being his dirty little secret."

"Agreed," Natalie says immediately. "That's not okay. He needs to stand up to the studio and make it clear that they don't get to dictate who he's seen with. I've heard of them doing those things before. I know that Luke had to deal with some of that, and after he put his foot down, he was much happier.

"Also, you need to know that most of what you'll see or read about him is completely untrue. And if you don't listen to him and trust him, it could ruin your relationship quickly."

"In what way?"

This is freaking fascinating! I'm so happy that Luke and Natalie came to visit, not only because they're nice people and I've enjoyed getting to know them, but because Natalie is the only person in the world I know who *gets it.*

"Okay, get this." She leans forward. "Not long after Luke and I were together, he had to go to L.A. for something. I forget what. But while he was gone, I got super sick and had to go to the hospital.

"So, I'm in the hospital room, *so sick*, and my best friend Jules is with me. The TV is on, and suddenly, there's Luke, with some other famous movie star, and it looks like they're super cozy with each other."

"Oh, God." I cover my mouth in horror. "That's horrible."

"Want to know the worst part? I'd just found out I was freaking *pregnant.*"

"No."

"Oh, yes. So, I'm sitting there, sick as a dog and pregnant with this guy's baby, and as far as I know, he's canoodling with some Hollywood bimbo."

"But it worked out."

"It did." She nods happily. "The press will spin *everything*. They always make it look worse than it is. Luke warned me from the beginning to listen to him. That if I had a question, to go directly to him. But in that moment, I didn't listen, and I assumed that we were through."

"Oh, Natalie."

"It was a tough time. But it worked out, and here we are, almost six years and four kids later."

"That's a lot of kids in six years."

She laughs. "Oh, girl, you're not kidding. But he's such a *good* daddy, and he loves me more than anything in this world. The rest of it? Well, it feeds his soul, too. So sometimes we have to compromise, but at the end of the day, the kids and I have Luke, and I wouldn't trade that for anything."

"I love your love," I say with a dreamy sigh. "I admit, I've had a crush on your husband since I was a teenager."

"You and many thousands of other girls."

"I love that he's a good husband and father. That I didn't have a crush on a creep. And that he found you."

"Thank you. I think that Christian and Luke have a lot in common. You'll have to be patient with him, Jenna. He's figuring this all out, and if he's anything like Luke was when I first met him, there's a lot about this business that hurts him."

"I think you're right." I swallow around the tears trying to form. "I see a struggle in him."

"You're both going to be so great. Each of you is a fantastic catch. And this may be because I'm biased, but I think it works out best for them when they're with someone who isn't already part of that crazy world."

"That makes sense. Natalie, thank you for this. I needed it."

"I know." She reaches over to take my hand. "If you ever need to talk or vent or just bounce something off someone, just call me. We are part of a very exclusive club."

"I'm not exactly part of that club yet," I reply with a laugh. "He's only here for a few weeks."

"I knew I loved Luke after the first week," she says with a wink. "Time doesn't matter, Jenna. Sometimes, you meet someone, and you just know. It's like an instant recognition. Like your heart is saying, *oh, there you are.*"

"Don't make me cry." I sniff. "I don't know what's going to happen, but I care about him, and I know that I don't want to overthink it."

"Good plan. In fact, *don't overthink it* should be your new motto."

I take a deep breath and check the time.

"Oh, we should get going. You and Luke have to catch a flight this afternoon."

"It's Luke's plane, so we can leave anytime. But you're right, I'm ready to get home to my babies."

Once we've changed into our clothes and gathered our things, we walk out to the receptionist to pay.

I pull out my debit card, but the receptionist just smiles and passes me a huge bouquet of pink roses with a note.

I hope you had a lovely time.

<3 – C

"Yeah, he's not in it for the long haul at all," Natalie says and gives me a wink as she offers her card to the receptionist. "That's one romantic man you have there."

"Yours is also taken care of," Natalie is told. "You ladies are good to go."

"Looks like we both have romantic men."

***

"I don't want to get up," I whisper into Christian's ear the next morning. "It's so warm and comfy here."

I'm spooned up behind him, enjoying him. He smells like his shower gel with a tiny bit of sweat mixed in from last night's sexcapades. His back and shoulders are…*yum.* I love trailing my tongue along his spine, where the muscles dip in. And he's naked, so my hands can roam all over his warm skin with a pause on his firm ass.

The man is firm everywhere.

Every. Where.

"You don't have to get up." He turns onto his back, making me stick my lower lip out in a pout. "We can stay here all day if you want to. Why are you pouting?"

He tickles my lip with his finger.

"You took your butt away, and I'm rather fond of it."

"Poor baby." He wraps those muscular arms around me and pulls me in for a hug.

I didn't realize until I met Christian that naked hugs are my jam.

His lips find my neck, and goosebumps immediately cover my skin from head to toe. His hands move from my neck to the small of my back, and the next thing I know, he's flipped us so he's hovering over me, kissing my collarbones, and grazing those magical fingertips over my nipples.

My whole body is now fully awake and ready for action. If I were wearing panties, they'd be soaked.

Or incinerated.

"Do you know what you do to me?" he asks, licking the underside of my small breast. The skin there is thin and ultra-sensitive, and I can't help but circle my hips in invitation.

"What's that?" I breathe, burying my fingers in his soft hair.

"Well, there's a list," he begins and drags his tongue down my sternum. "You make me hard."

He presses his cock to my inner thigh and glances up at me with devilish, lust-filled, blue eyes.

"You make me smile," he adds and circles his nose around my belly button. I catch my breath and bite my lip, so turned on that I don't know what to do with myself. So, I fist the sheets and hold on tight.

"Grip onto me like that," he says, and I do. I hold onto his shoulders with all my might, unable to do anything else as his mouth wreaks havoc on my body. His fingers are still strumming over my nipples as he kisses his way down my pubis to the most sensitive part of me.

"You make me forget things," he says, surprising me. "And you make me want things that I never have before."

I don't have time to ask him what he means by that before he plants those delicious lips on my clit and kisses me there, and my body erupts with pure, unadulterated pleasure.

I cry out, but it doesn't stop him. He pushes two fingers into me, makes that incredible *come here* motion, and I shatter, twisting in the sheets and fisting his hair in my hands as orgasm after orgasm rolls through me.

Finally, he kisses his way up my body and, with his mouth on mine, he sinks inside me, then stops and just stares down at me.

I swear, I can't breathe when he looks at me like this. Like I'm the only thing he sees.

My God, I've fallen in love with Christian Wolfe. Irrevocably, unequivocally in love with him.

"Condom," he says, suddenly horrified. "Fuck, I forgot."

I sweep his hair off his forehead. "I'm on the pill," I whisper. He blinks rapidly and shakes his head.

"I *never* forget. I'm sorry, Jenna."

"We're safe," I repeat and brush my fingers down his cheek as he kisses me soundly. I can taste myself on him, and that only fuels my need.

I need him.

He links his fingers with mine and pins that hand over my head, then begins to move over me, inside me, watching me with fierce, blue eyes.

It's the most intense sex I've ever had in my life.

"You make me want things," he whispers again before tracing those lips over my cheek to my ear. He's moving faster, and I hitch my legs up around his hips, opening myself to him more, wanting to feel every single inch of him.

God, he fills me completely. Not just physically, but he fills my heart, too.

He scares the shit out of me.

"Stop thinking," he says before pulling my nipple between his lips and giving it a tug. "Just feel, Jenna."

"Oh, I feel you."

I reach down and cup his ass, loving the way the hard muscle feels as he flexes, moving in and out of me.

What I wouldn't give for a mirror right now.

"Jesus, babe," he growls. "I can't hold on."

"Don't hold on." I grip his dick tighter and watch in wonderment as he clenches his eyes shut, succumbing to his own orgasm. Every muscle in his body tenses. He quivers.

He leans in and bites my shoulder, which only makes me contract around him more.

"Fucking hell," he murmurs.

"Mm." I kiss his neck, and then his cheek. "Good morning."

"The best morning I've had in a while." He props himself on his elbows and smiles down at me. "How are you?"

"Happy. Satiated. Not caffeinated."

He laughs and kisses me, then rolls away and rubs his hands over his face.

"I do need to get up," I say with a sigh. "I need to get my stuff together and go home now that my house is put back together."

"No way." He snags me around the waist and

pulls me against him again, holding me prisoner and making me giggle.

"I do need clean clothes, you know. And I have some things to check on."

He sighs and kisses the ball of my shoulder, reawakening parts of my body that I would have sworn were satiated.

"I know you have a life, and things to tend to," he says. "But I only have two more weeks here. Spend your nights with me."

He turns me to face him, looking me in the eyes. "I want to spend every minute that I can with you. We'll both be working during the day, but I want you here, in my bed, at night."

How in the hell do I say no to that?

I don't *want* to say no to that.

So, instead, I kiss him and then wrap my arms around his neck and hug him tightly.

Two weeks.

That's all we have, and then what?

"I would love that." I kiss his cheek again and then tear myself away. "But I do need some things from my house, and I need food."

"And coffee," he says with a grin.

I stand and look back at him. He's still lying there, his arms crossed behind his head, looking all rumpled and fresh.

Sexier than should be legal.

"All the coffee," I agree. "Oh, and I was going to tell you, the Christmas Stroll in downtown Cunningham Falls is tonight, and I'll be going with Hannah and Brad. Would you like to come?"

He's still smiling.

"You can wear a hat and a coat so you'll be sort of disguised, and not a lot of tourists go to this anyway. It's not supposed to be too cold. There's food and vendors, and the shops are open with sales going on."

"It sounds like fun."

I smile, as excited as if he just said I won the lottery. "Yeah? Cool. I'll even buy you a souvenir, so you have something to remind you of your time here."

His face sobers, and he reaches up, grabs my arm, and pulls me back into bed.

"What did I say?"

"Let's not talk about when I leave anymore, okay?"

"You brought it up."

"And I'm asking to drop it." He kisses my forehead. "I'd love to go to the stroll with you guys. It'll be great. And then I want to take you to bed and make love to you all night long."

"I'm going to be really tired after that."

He smiles and rubs his nose against mine. "I plan to keep you permanently tired."

"I'm a lucky girl."

CHAPTER TEN

Jenna

IT'S CHILLY TONIGHT, but the cold air feels good against my cheeks. The air smells fresh, with a hint of hot cider coming from one of the vendors.

"So, they block off Main Street for this," Christian says, munching on a cookie.

"Yep. Don't you feel like a rebel, walking down the middle of the street?"

He smiles down at me. "If this is as rebellious as you get, I think you're going to be just fine."

"Are you teasing me?"

"Oh, yeah," he says with a laugh. His ski instructor, Chad Holmes, waves at us from across the street then jogs over to join us.

"Hey there."

"Hi, Chad."

"Jenna, you have to see this," Hannah says,

pulling me away. I leave Christian and Chad to their conversation so I can check out the clothes racks that Willa's pulled outside of her shop, Dress It Up. "Look at this dress. It's fifty percent off."

"It's totally your color." I run the green cotton through my fingers. "And it's so soft. You have to snag it."

"You're right." She throws it over her arm, and we continue to thumb through the racks.

"Hello, ladies," Willa says as she comes outside carrying a tray of plastic champagne glasses full of sparkly, bubbly goodness. "I know others are serving hot wine, but come on. We need bubbly."

"Can't argue with that," I agree and take a glass.

"I'm on call tonight," Hannah replies. "With my luck, someone will go into labor, and I'll have to jet."

"I brought you the non-alcoholic variety," Willa says with a wink, pointing to one of the glasses. "Just for you."

"You're the best," Hannah says with an excited little dance. "And you've seriously outdone yourself here, Willa. Your shop is gorgeous, all decorated up for the holidays."

"I love Christmas. After the accident, I didn't want to celebrate it anymore, but I have a little boy who loves the wonderment of it all, so we do it up big."

"Good for you," I reply and then watch her

eyes widen. I feel Christian walk up behind me, can feel the heat from him against my back. "Willa, this is Christian Wolfe."

"Not a doppelganger, then," she says with a laugh and accepts his outstretched hand to shake. "I'm Willa. Nice to meet you."

"Likewise," Christian says with a nod.

"This is Willa's store, and it's absolutely brilliant," I say as Hannah excitedly holds up another find. "You need that."

"I totally do." She passes all of her finds to Brad, who's also joined us.

"Are we getting all of this?" Brad asks.

"Yep. You're my Sherpa."

They both laugh as they move inside to keep shopping, and Willa offers Christian a glass of champagne.

"Let me know if you need anything," she says and gives me a look that says *we need to talk about this STAT.*

I wink at her and sip my bubbly, turning to the man himself. He's in jeans and boots, has a grey ski jacket over his layers to keep him warm, and a grey hat. His face is still a bit stubbled, and I want to reach up and tickle it, but I don't.

No affection in public.

So far, only people he has actually met and my friends have approached us. I don't know if anyone else has recognized him, but if they have, they've left us alone.

It's freaking awesome, and as every minute passes, I can feel him start to relax. His broad shoulders have dropped a bit, and he's quick to smile.

His eyes still shift a little, taking in our surroundings, but he's paying attention to conversations around us rather than focusing on the crowd.

"Is that the Willa you referenced when you were talking to Max the other day?" he asks.

"Yep." I watch her make her rounds, offering drinks and advice to her customers. "I've known her since we were toddlers. She's a year older than me, and she and Max were an item all through high school."

"It's cool that you're still friends."

"There are days I like her better than I do Max," I say with a laugh. "And, frankly, I never would have chosen between them. There weren't sides to take, no one did anything wrong necessarily. Except, my brother is stupid."

"He must have broken it off." He takes my empty glass and sets it and his on a table that Willa set out just for that.

"He did. He wanted to go away to college and see the world, and for Willa, her world was right here in Cunningham Falls."

Christian nods. "Shall we stroll?"

"We shall." We walk down the sidewalk, checking out food being sampled or sold, looking over knickknacks and listening to music. "Thank God you don't touch me in public."

His gaze whips down to me. "What? Why?"

"Because knowing you, you'd whisk me into a dance, right here on Main Street in front of most of the people I know, and I can't dance."

"You can, too," he says, shaking his head. "And you don't know that I'd do that."

"You're already tapping your toe and nodding your head. You want to dance."

A slow smile spreads over that handsome face. "I could dance with you here."

"Nope." I laugh and adjust my hat. "You don't do that in public, so I'm safe."

Is that hurt in my voice? If it is, it's ridiculous because I definitely *don't* want to dance with him right here and now.

But I'd love it if he held my hand or put his palm on the small of my back.

Or *something.*

But this is Christian, and he's careful. And I need to respect that, even if I don't love it.

"Look at me."

I comply. The fire roasting chestnuts to our left is reflected in his eyes, over his face. It's warmer here, and not just because of the flames.

"Hey, you two!"

We're interrupted by Ed, the owner of Ed's Diner, and the moment is lost.

"Hi, Ed." I smile at the older man as he claps Christian on the shoulder. "They let you get away from the food truck for a bit?"

"I don't actually man it much these days," he says with a smile. "I have people for that."

"You let someone else touch your grill?"

"A man has to retire sometime," he replies with a wink. "How are you two?"

"We're enjoying the festivities," Christian replies. "And I have to thank you for that delicious breakfast the other day."

"You'll have to visit us again. I promise there won't be a repeat of last time." Ed smiles kindly. "You two have a good evening."

He walks away, and I nudge Christian with my elbow. "Look at you, turning into a local. You know almost as many people here as I do."

"I think that's an exaggeration," he says with a laugh as we continue walking down the street. "But I do like the people here."

"It's a nice town," I agree. "And I'm not just saying that because I'm biased."

"You're biased," he says and nudges me now. "But you should be."

I shrug and glance down at my feet. Suddenly, Christian takes my hand, surprising me, and pulls me to the edge of the sidewalk, pressing my back to a column.

"What are you doing?"

"Look up."

Mistletoe.

I raise a brow. "Well, look at that."

He leans in, his eyes trained on my lips. I wet them as he slides one hand to my hip and the other cups my cheek, his thumb circling the apple.

"I want to touch you *everywhere*," he whispers. "Even in public."

And with that, he presses his lips to mine. He doesn't deepen the kiss, but he doesn't pull away in a quick peck either.

And I swear to God, the earth falls out from under me.

After what feels like minutes, but is only a couple of seconds, he pulls back and smiles down at me.

"Let's go home."

***

He kissed me, in front of the whole town of Cunningham Falls. Granted, I don't think more than a handful of people saw it, but he did it all the same.

And it made me feel special. Important.

That's all I ever wanted.

It's the next morning, after a long night of intense love-making, and I'm in the kitchen of my house in town, getting breakfast underway while

Christian takes a shower.

If I let myself dwell on the fact that Christian is naked and wet in my bathroom, I won't get anything done, so I turn on my favorite Spotify playlist on my phone, connect it to the speakers that I have wired through the whole house, and set to work while dancing to Ed Sheeran.

"I'm in love with the shape of you..."

I'm singing under my breath as I crack eggs into a bowl and whisk them up, then do a little sashay to the fridge for some milk and butter.

Knowing that I'm alone, I let my hips move, shake my shoulders, and do a little bounce back to the bowl of eggs.

"Wow."

I jump and spin, letting out a surprised squeak.

"Oh, you startled me."

"I'm so proud of you. Look at you, dancing and everything."

"I didn't know I had an audience," I reply, my hand pressed to my chest, willing my heart to slow down, but Christian's looking at me as though he'd like to eat me alive, and that's not something that'll slow down a girl's heart rate.

He's in sweatpants that are slung low on his hips, showing off that sexy V and his abs because the man isn't wearing a shirt.

"I love this song," he says, slowly walking to me, in the rhythm of the music. His hips are moving now, and he holds his hand out for mine.

"No."

"Don't stop now," he says and pulls me into his arms, then spins me out and back to him. But it's not like the dancing we did before.

His posture isn't perfect. He's not holding me at a respectable distance.

No, he's all over me, moving around me, his hips and shoulders pressed to mine as he spins us in a sensual dance that has my nipples perked up and my clean panties soaked.

He turns me and presses his front to my back, still turning us in circles, but now he can press his mouth to my neck, just under my ear.

"I'm in love with your body…"

Truer words have never been spoken.

Or sung.

"See what happens when you let your body go?" he asks against my skin. "When you forget to worry about if you look silly? You don't, by the way."

"Next to you, a professional dancer?"

He kisses that sensitive spot, just under my ear.

"It doesn't matter, Jenna. Doesn't matter if you've been to a thousand dance classes or none at all, as long as you feel the music and the person you're dancing with."

He turns me back around to face him and cups

my cheek, just the way he did last night and lowers his lips to mine. He doesn't miss a step, still moving us about the kitchen.

And I'm completely intoxicated by him, caught up in the way he moves, the way he smells, and absolutely enraptured by the way he's looking at me.

"Just watch my face, feel my body. No matter how we're dancing. Fast, slow, or even having sex, that's the trick."

"There are tricks to sex?"

He laughs and twirls me effortlessly.

"I'm not going to teach you to count steps. It's not fun, and you won't ever have to use it."

"No? What if I'm called to be the lead in a dance recital?"

His lips twitch. "Does that happen often?"

"We don't know. It *could* happen."

"Well, if it does, I'll be happy to be your private coach," he replies, wiggling his eyebrows. "And I'll be in the front row, cheering you on."

"Like a dance mom," I agree, nodding with sarcastic enthusiasm that makes him bust out laughing. But then he pulls me close into a tight hug as the song changes to a slow P!nk song, and he slows our movements with the beat of the music.

"I don't want you to think that I don't want to touch you when we're not in our bubble," he says, holding my gaze intently. He leads me to the kitchen table, boosts me onto it, and cages me there, his hands on either side of my hips. He's gone from playful to intense in two-point-six seconds.

"Christian, it's okay."

"No." He bumps my nose with his. "It's not okay. I don't *ever* want you to feel that you're insignificant or less than. That you're not important."

I feel tears prick my eyes, and I reach up to brush them away, but he beats me to it and then kisses the outer edges of my eyes.

My God, I love him so much my heart aches with it.

"Neither of us deserves it," I whisper, pressing my hands to his sides. "It's not just me."

"I know," he says. "I'll figure it out, and I'm apologizing for the mess that is my public life. We should eat. I need to talk to you."

"The eggs are ready; all I have to do is whip up the omelets."

"That easy, huh?" he asks as he pulls away, and I jump off the table.

"It is pretty easy, actually."

He makes himself a cup of coffee as I get the omelets underway, and when we're sitting at the table, digging into our food, he looks up at me in surprise.

"This is really good."

"I wasn't going to serve you something that isn't good."

He laughs and takes another bite of his eggs. "Now that I know you're this good of a cook, I'll coerce you into cooking for me more often."

"I've cooked for you several times."

He grins that cocky, confident smile that makes me want to lean in and kiss it right off him.

So, I do.

And when I pull away, I'm satisfied to find that his eyes have dilated, and he's breathing just a bit harder.

"Okay, what do you want to talk about?" I take a bite of my toast, then reach for the strawberry jam my mom made last summer when she and Dad were here from Arizona.

"My job." He takes a sip of coffee out of my *Sorry I'm late, I didn't want to come* mug.

It makes me giggle.

"My job is funny?"

"No, that mug is funny. Sorry. Talk to me."

"The press is vicious," he begins, as calmly as if he's chatting about the eggs on his plate. "They spin stories, and they make *everything* look like a scandal. I wore Adidas rather than Nike? Well, shit, my Nike contract must be over."

"Do you have a Nike contract?" I ask.

"No, that's just an example."

"Gotcha. But if you *do* get a Nike contract, hook a girl up."

He shakes his head, watching me with a crooked smile. "You're not taking this seriously."

"I am." I push my empty plate away and reach for my *Please do not pet the peeves* mug of coffee. "Christian, I spoke with Natalie the other day, and I've been doing a lot of thinking. Your career is important to you, just like mine is to me. I respect it, and even if I don't always agree with it, I will *always* respect it.

"That means that I also have to take a lot of it in stride, and I need to trust you. Nat told me some horror stories about the press and Luke, and she also spoke some truth to me. I'm not a jealous woman, and I'm not irrational."

"So, you're an enigma," he says, his eyes narrowed.

"No, I'm not a drama queen." I wink at him and take another sip of coffee. "That doesn't mean you get to kiss all the girls, though."

"Damn." He sighs and tosses his fork down in a clatter, making me jump and then laugh. "My plan has been foiled again."

"Yep."

"I do have to kiss girls and sometimes more than that in the movies I do," he reminds me, and I frown.

"Huh. I hadn't thought of that."

"You should think of it. You should think about all of it before this goes any further because it's not easy. It's not simple. And while I do make a lot of money and I can do fun things, and I'm devastatingly handsome—"

I snort, and he narrows his eyes at me again.

"—there may come a time when you just don't want to deal with it anymore."

"I've been warned," I reply, then lean over to kiss him. "Thanks for warning me."

"Take it seriously," he says and tucks my hair behind my ear, sending sparks tingling down my arm. Then he takes my hand and gives it a squeeze.

I want to ask him if he's telling me all of this because he plans to be with me past when he leaves in two weeks. I want to tell him that none of it matters.

But I know that's a lie.

It matters.

"I do take it seriously, and I'll consider everything you've said."

He nods and kisses my hand. "Thank you."

"What should we do today? Do you want to watch some movies here at the house?"

"Yes, I absolutely want to watch movies," he says with a nod. "I'll pick, and then you pick."

"What if what you pick sucks?"

He glares at me as his phone rings.

"You're sassy today."

I shrug one shoulder, and he accepts the call, then puts it on speaker.

"Hey, Nina. What's up?"

"What the fuck did you do, Christian?"

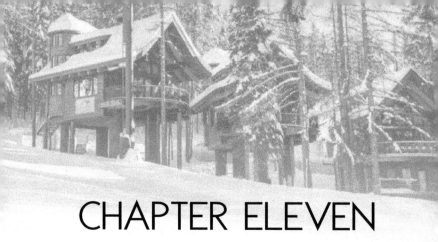

CHAPTER ELEVEN

Christian

I SCOWL, STARING AT Jenna, who is frowning back at me.

"What are you talking about?"

"Get your computer out," Nina replies.

"I'm not near my computer."

"I'll get mine," Jenna says and jumps up to fetch her laptop.

"Is that her?" Nina asks.

"To which *her* are you referring, exactly?"

Nina sighs loudly, and she's on my very last nerve.

"Here." Jenna sets the computer on the table in front of me and leans over me to type in her password and bring up her browser.

"Go to TMZ, that'll be fastest," Nina says, and my stomach drops, dread filling me. I type in the site, and right there, front and center is not just a photo.

No, that would be too easy to dismiss.

They have video.

"Press play," Nina says simply.

"Oh, my God," Jenna says from next to me.

"Is that her, Christian?" Nina asks.

"Shut up, Nina." I press play on the video, and sure enough. There we are, Jenna and I at the stroll last night. It's when I kiss her under the mistletoe. The video keeps going as I end the kiss and we walk down the street away from the camera. "Okay, I've seen it."

"I can't *even* believe you did this," Nina begins, and I sit back, rub my fingers over my eyes, and then reach for Jenna's hand. She's cold. Her face is pale, and her eyes are full of regret.

And that's the last fucking thing I ever want to see from her.

"I mean, seriously. You are never this careless. You're seriously letting a snow bunny fuck everything up for you?"

"Whoa," I reply, leaning in so she can hear me crystal-clear. "One, I'm not stupid, and I'm not careless, certainly not enough to screw anything up over someone I don't give a shit about. Two, Jenna isn't a snow bunny.

"And three, you may be my sister, but you best remember that you're my *employee*. You work for me. So watch your fucking tone with me, Nina."

"I'm going to go get some laundry done," Jenna says quietly, then kisses my cheek and walks out of the room.

I've never been angrier with Nina in my life, and I want nothing more than to follow Jenna, pull her to me, hold her, and reassure us both.

But this little hiccup needs to be dealt with first.

"I'm getting bombarded with messages and calls," Nina says. "So is the whole social media team. Grant will be calling in a few, I'm sure."

Grant Hollis is my agent, and I have no doubts that he'll be buzzing through any second.

"I need to know if we're going to release a formal statement."

"And say what?" I stand to pace the kitchen and living room. "That I can't stand Serena, have never dated her even once, and I'm falling for a landlord in Montana?"

"You're *falling for her*?" Nina's voice is full of shock and dismay. "Jesus, Chris, you were supposed to go learn how to ski, bang a few girls, and come home refreshed. Not get attached. This can't work."

"*This* is none of your damn business," I reply.

"Wrong. It *is* my business because I'm the one in L.A. cleaning up your mess. What were you thinking? You're never careless. Unless you count the DUI, but I'm choosing not to."

"I was thinking that there was mistletoe, and the girl I'm crazy about was conveniently under it." I shove my hand through my hair. "I'm allowed to be a man, Nina."

"Not in this business." She sounds distracted as if she's reading something. "*People* magazine just reached out for a comment. And this will be all over *Entertainment Tonight* this afternoon."

"I don't care."

"You'd better care, big brother. Because you're about to start promoting a movie, and part of that is promoting it *with* Serena."

"Awesome." I walk back to the bathroom and reach for my T-shirt, tugging it over my head as I march back to the computer and start to Google it. "I hate that they call her the *other woman*."

"As far as anyone knows, she is," Nina reminds me. "I know it sucks. I don't like Serena either. She's a bitch."

"What if we ignore it?"

She's quiet for a moment, and I expect her to explode. But I'm surprised.

"It's not like you can deny that it's you," she says quietly. "Give me a minute, I'm thinking."

"Let's be real here. We could spin it as it being a secret project that I'm filming. There are a million things to say."

But none of those protect and show respect to Jenna, who has quickly come to be the most important part of my damn life.

Everything about this makes me feel like a creepy asshole.

"True," Nina says. "I kind of like that."

"Actually, scratch that. I'm done lying, and Jenna is worth way more than lies."

"Christ, you've really got it bad for this girl."

"She's amazing, Nina, and I won't disrespect her by making it out to either be nothing at all or something dirty. So, for now, we don't say anything at all."

"The speculation, Christian—"

"Guess how many fucks I give about speculation?"

She sighs and hangs up without saying goodbye, which doesn't surprise me in the least. Just as I'm about to go in search of Jenna to try and smooth things over, Grant calls through.

"Hey."

"From the tone of your voice," he begins, "I assume you've already seen the media shitstorm."

I sigh and pinch the bridge of my nose. I feel a headache coming on. Jenna walks into the room and passes me two Advil with a bottle of water, offers me a small smile, and walks back out again.

God, I love her.

"I've seen it," I confirm.

Grant's been with me since day one, through

the lean years and the times we could hardly keep up with. He is one of a handful of people that I trust implicitly.

"I need to know what you want me to tell the studio," he says with a sigh. "And before you do, I have something to say."

"I will not apologize."

"I don't want a fucking apology," he says, and I can just picture the frown on his wrinkled face, those bushy eyebrows pulled together. "I say it's about time you started living your life for *you*. It's not in your contract that you have to date your co-star. They can't require it anymore."

"It's fucking crazy that they ever did."

"They did a lot of crazy things," he says. "You don't know the half of it. My point is, I'll tell them whatever you want me to. I'm just happy to see you living your life, Christian. You've spent the better part of twenty-five years as a damn robot, and it's time to stop that."

"Are you telling me to stop working?"

"Fuck, no. I need to send one more kid to college."

I grin, knowing that he's not kidding in the least.

"I told Nina not to say anything at all, to not release an official statement. I want *you* to tell the studio that I'll do the press junket with Serena, and I'll play nice, but I don't like her, and I won't pretend to be dating her. The film is finished, and that's all that matters."

"I like it," he says. "They won't, but I do."

"Honestly, I don't care whether they like it or not. Not anymore. It's too much, Grant."

"I completely agree, and we'll be completely transparent moving forward regarding this. Date whomever you want, kiddo. Just don't get her pregnant and leave her and let her go on a shitty reality show."

I laugh in spite of myself and cover my mouth with my hand. "Jesus, that's quite the visual."

"Hey, that's sound advice. Okay, I'll make some calls. Enjoy your girl. Let me know when you're back in town."

"Thanks, Grant."

I hang up, leave my phone in the kitchen and on silent because I don't want to deal with this anymore today, and go in search of my girl.

I lean my shoulder against the doorjamb of her bedroom and cross my arms over my chest, watching her.

She's sitting in the middle of her bed, her legs folded up under her, intently watching her phone. She taps the screen, and I can hear the video from the stroll playing. When it's over, she plays it again.

After the third time, I push away from the doorway and walk toward her.

"Jenna."

She looks up at me with shining blue eyes, tears

threatening, and my heart sinks.

"Sweetheart, I'm so sorry."

"I kind of love this video."

I stop short, completely stunned by this admission.

"You do?"

She nods and brushes a tear off of her cheek. "I know that it's causing problems for you and I'm sorry for that. But, Christian, this was one of the most romantic moments in my life, and someone caught it on film."

She offers me a small smile, then plays it again. I sit next to her, watching over her shoulder as I lean in and kiss her on the screen.

You can't hear what I say to her, thank God, because I want that to always stay between us. But I have to admit, it's good quality, and it's sweet.

"You're not angry?" I ask her.

"Isn't it ironic that we literally *just* finished having a conversation about this very thing happening?" she asks rather than answering my question. "I'm not angry. I'm saving this to my phone so I can watch it whenever I want to."

It occurs to me that she and I have never taken a photo together. After that first encounter in the coffee shop, when she took a photo of her coffee, and I shied away, she's never tried to take another one of anything.

That's about to change.

Whether we only have a couple of weeks or fifty years together, I want us both to have the memories.

***

"So, all of this is CGI," Jenna says as we're snuggled up on the couch of my tree house later that night watching *Iron Man*.

"Most of it."

"That must be hard for an actor to not actually work with other actors."

I kiss her temple. I love that she's starting to pick apart some of the art of it to try and see it from my eyes, but at the same time, I don't want her to lose the wonderment of movies.

"You get used to it," I reply simply.

"That Robert Downey, Jr. gets better with age," she says and eats some popcorn.

"He's nice, too."

Her gaze whips up to mine. "You *know* him?"

"I've met him a few times, yes."

"Wow."

I laugh now and kiss her again. "And here I am, reminding you yet again, that some people think it's impressive that Robert knows *me*."

"Oh, stop. You don't need an ego boost." She pats my knee and opens her phone, looking all over Instagram and the gossip sites to see what's being said this evening.

"You shouldn't look at that shit."

"It's fascinating," she says, reaching for some Twizzlers. "There are polls up now to ask people if they think that you or Serena cheated first."

"Hmm."

I'm annoyed. Not at her. Jenna didn't do anything wrong. I just hate public speculation. It's why I've always played by the rules.

"Oh!" She sits up and points at her screen. "Serena released a statement!"

"Oh, goodie."

She snorts and then clears her throat, reading aloud. "It's with the utmost regret that I confirm that Christian and I have decided to go separate ways. I have the utmost respect for him as an artist, and as a person, and we will continue to stay friends."

Jenna frowns. "Did no one proofread this for her? She used *utmost* twice."

I laugh and shrug. "Who knows? Maybe she threw it out there herself at the last minute."

"Maybe." She settles against me again and continues to page through her phone. "Wow, there are a lot of photos of her out there with other men. Some of them posted in the last couple of weeks while she was supposedly still with you."

She glances up at me and frowns.

"Serena likes men."

She likes women, too, but we won't go there.

"But no one said anything about it. There wasn't a media shitstorm until it was *you*."

I shrug again, mostly because I'm not exactly sure what to say.

"Why?" she asks.

"Serena has only been in the public eye for a couple of years. She's relatively new to the business."

"So?"

"Look, I'm not trying to sound full of myself here, but she's not exactly as...*famous* as I am. That was one of the reasons that we were always paired up, and it was made to look like we were together."

"To make her more famous?" Her jaw drops, and she stares at me for a moment. "No way."

"Way."

"Well, that's stupid. She should be successful off of her own merit, not because she's on your arm."

She sits forward, and I have a feeling this has pushed one of Jenna's buttons.

"You know," she continues, "this is bullshit, and it pisses me right off."

"I can see that."

"Women complain about not getting the same opportunities as men, not getting the same pay, all of those things. And I *agree* with those things, don't get me wrong. But then something like this happens, where a woman is using her looks, her connections, to get ahead, and it's like setting the women's lib movement back fifty years."

"Interesting."

"I'm serious, Christian. That's the most ridiculous thing I've ever heard, and she should be ashamed of herself. That's not a work ethic."

Look at her. She's fucking amazing.

"Easy there, tiger."

She scowls and then sighs and collapses against me.

"I can't change it," she says with a sigh. "I just don't like it when people use someone else to get where they want to go, and that's exactly what she did to you."

I bury my lips in her hair, brushing them back and forth, breathing her in.

"I guess I hadn't thought of it like that."

"It happens to Max, too. I'm sure it happens to most people, in all kinds of careers. It's dumb. I'm a fan of a strong work ethic."

"It's one of the things I admire about you." I pull her close and sigh when she wraps her arms around my torso, hugging me tightly. "You're a fierce woman, and it's fucking fantastic."

"Well. What's the point of being anything else?"

I smile as she turns up the volume on the movie. We are quiet as the show finishes, curled up together while it silently snows outside. The media means absolutely nothing.

Nothing.

I can't say that I'm not ready to get back to work because acting is what feeds my soul, but being here with Jenna also feeds me in ways that I didn't know I was lacking.

I feel at home here, and I don't know if I've ever truly felt that way anywhere before, aside from on a stage or a movie set.

It seems that Jenna is what I've been searching for my whole life, and now that I've found her, how do I keep her?

She's breathing evenly, so I lean forward to check on her and, sure enough, she's fallen asleep against my chest. I turn off the TV and lift her easily. She wraps her sweet arms around my neck and buries her face against my chest as I carry her around the tree house, turning off lights and making sure the door is locked before I take her to bed.

I'd planned to make love to her again tonight, but she's exhausted, and if I'm being honest, so am I. It was a trying day.

One I'm ready to be over.

Once I tuck Jenna into bed, I make a trip to the bathroom and take a quick, hot shower to wash the rest of the day away. When I return to the bed, Jenna is curled up in the middle of it, her legs tucked up to her chest, and her sweet lips tipped up.

I wonder what she's dreaming of?

I slip in next to her, and she immediately seeks me out, wrapping herself around me. Sleep hovers around my mind, closing in on the worries from to-day, and before long, I'm sleeping with her, tucked safely in the trees and snow of Cunningham Falls.

CHAPTER TWELVE

Jenna

"**T**HANKS FOR STAYING WITH US," I say to the older Canadian couple who came down to spend the week in the Ponderosa with their family. "I hope you enjoyed yourself."

"We did," the wife says with a wink. "And we'll be back next year."

"Excellent. Drive safely."

I wave them off and walk into the unit and do a quick walk-through to make sure there's no damage.

I wouldn't expect a nice family to destroy anything, but I've learned the hard way that it can—and does—happen.

Thankfully, the tree house only requires a good scrubbing, not new drywall.

My phone rings in my pocket. "Hello?"

"Hey, famous friend," Willa says. I can hear the smile in her voice. "You didn't tell me that you and Christian are an item."

"There's a long conversation over wine needed very soon," I reply as I lock the Ponderosa behind me and walk over to Christian's unit. He's skiing now but should be back any time.

"Oh, yes. And the sooner, the better," she agrees. "I'm actually not calling to give you shit about your love life."

"Oh, good."

"I'm calling to remind you that we're doing our annual girlfriend gift exchange tomorrow night."

"I wouldn't forget that. It's one of my favorite nights of the year."

"Me, too. We've changed the location from Hannah's to Grace's house."

I frown as I pull a bottle of water from the fridge. "Any particular reason?"

"She just has more space," she says, but I don't think that's the whole truth. Before I can ask any other questions, though, she says, "Alex just got home from school, so I have to jet. I'll see you tomorrow night at Grace's."

And with that, she hangs up.

It doesn't really matter to me where we have it, as long as it isn't cancelled. We've done this for years, buying small gifts for each other and having a party before Christmas to exchange them and enjoy our friendships.

Plus, I love giving presents, and I can't wait until they see what I got them this year.

"Honey, I'm home," Christian says in his best Ricky Ricardo voice from the front door. He shuffles around for a bit, shedding his gear, and then strolls into the living room and leans over the couch to kiss me soundly. I grab onto his shoulders and pull him over onto me, making us both laugh.

But it totally works to initiate a hot make-out session.

"How are you?" he asks when he comes up for air. I didn't see him this morning because he left for his ski session before I woke up.

"I'm good." I brush his hair off his forehead. It's getting longer, and I think it's sexy when it's all mussed up from my fingers. "How was your day?"

"Cold and snowy," he says then pushes off me and walks to the kitchen to brew himself some coffee. "Did the guests in the Ponderosa leave this morning?"

I love that he listens. That he pays attention and takes an interest in my day.

"They did, and there's no permanent damage."

He cocks a brow. "Is that a surprise?"

"There were ten of them staying there if you count the kids, so I never know what I'll walk into. One of my houses downtown was missing drywall after a bachelor party came through, so I now have a strict policy of no bachelor parties, no Super Bowl parties, stuff like that. Hell, I'm not even excited when I hear there's going to be a baby shower in one of my units."

He sips his coffee and sits at the opposite end of the couch from me, so I put my feet in his lap, and he gives the arch of my foot a rub.

I might just purr.

"Have you heard any more from Nina today?" I ask.

"Nah, it's Sunday, so most people aren't in the office today. And I heard that there was a big scandal last night involving one of the Kardashians, so I think everyone has moved on."

"It's ridiculous, you know. The media frenzy."

He watches his hand move over my foot. "I know."

"I know I don't have a claim on you, and it's not my place to talk about this with you because I don't live it every day, and it's really none of my business, but I think that it's hard on you, and it seems to me that it could be hurtful. And I don't like that."

He looks up at me. "Thanks for that. I don't disagree."

I just nod, not sure of what else to say.

"Do you need anything?"

"Yes." I smile lazily at him. "If you don't mind getting cold again."

"How cold?"

I cringe. "Well, it's going to be pretty cold where we're going, but I'll bring hand and toe warmers, and we can sit in the hot tub later to warm up."

His eyes light up. "Naked hot tub sitting?"

"The other two units are empty tonight, so I don't see why not."

"Deal." He jumps up and starts pulling on his snow gear again, then pauses and frowns. "Where are we going?"

"Somewhere special."

***

"This is my favorite time of year in Glacier National Park," I inform him as I park my SUV where the road is blocked. "Don't get me wrong, it's always beautiful. And summer is spectacular because you can see more of it. Right now, most of the park is closed to visitors.

"But it's a trade-off because in the summer we have more than three million visitors to the area."

"Wow," he says as he pulls his gloves and hat on. "That's a lot of people."

"But right now, there's hardly anyone up here, and definitely not where we're going."

I smile and hop out of the car, circle around to the back, and open the hatchback.

"I have snowshoes for you," I inform him. "And poles."

"This is new," he says with interest and watches as I step into my snowshoes and fasten them. He does the same, and I get the car locked up, grab the supplies, and then stop to take a deep, cold breath.

"We only have to hike in half a mile, but it takes longer on three feet of snow."

He grins. "Lead the way."

I set off down the road that hasn't seen a plow in weeks. The evergreens are heavy with snow.

It looks like a movie.

Or a postcard.

"My property is back here," I inform him as I trudge through the snow. "I'll never be able to access it by road in the winter. They don't plow back here. But I'll get a sled, load it down with supplies, and pull it on a rope like this."

"That sounds like a crazy workout," he says. I turn back to look at him, amused that he hasn't even started to breathe hard. I know he could go faster than this, but he's patiently moving at my pace.

"It will be," I agree. "But so worth it. It stuns me that so many people are here in the summer months, and then I can come up here on days like today, and it's quiet. As perfectly quiet as you can get. Stop walking."

We pause in the middle of the road, the snow-laden trees towering around us.

It's completely silent. The only sound is my

heart in my ears and our slight breathing.

"I don't know if I've ever experienced anything like it," he says, his eyes pinned to mine.

"It's incredible," I whisper and wonder if we're still talking about our surroundings. "And at night, the darkness is absolute. There's no light noise. If you thought the stars and northern lights were incredible up at the tree houses, you'd be stunned to see them up here."

"You love it here."

I smile and turn to continue walking to my property.

"With my whole heart," I agree.

"Are there animals here?"

"Many." I shrug and keep going. "We have black bears and grizzly bears, although they're both sleeping now. Mountain lions, goats, elk, deer, moose, wolves—"

"Jesus," he mutters. "Are we going to need a gun?"

"I have one," I reply.

"Wait. You do?"

I turn to look at him. "I do. For animals, if I were to be attacked. Mostly by wolves, but a mountain lion isn't out of the question. The others most likely won't care that I'm here."

"You're kidding."

"Come on, city boy." I chuckle and lead him

off the road and down toward the shore of Lake McDonald. "My property line started at the road and comes all the way down to the lake. I have three acres."

"This is incredible."

I smile, pure joy bubbling up inside me as it always does when I'm here. This is truly my favorite place in the whole world.

It's warmer in the trees than down by the water, and the lake isn't completely frozen over. The edges are crusted with a light coating of ice.

There are animal tracks that lead down to the water. They look like deer tracks.

I lead Christian to the shoreline and set my pack down. He's standing, transfixed, looking at the mountains on the other side of the lake.

"Jenna," he says and swallows hard. "This is… unreal."

"It's real." I join him and slip my hand into his. "And this little piece of it is mine. It's everything that I want in the world, Christian. It's the perfect place."

He glances down at me. The tip of his nose is red from the cold, but it doesn't seem to bother him.

"Okay, let me show you my vision. You've seen the view, now turn and look at my vast property."

He does as I ask and leans on his pole. "Okay, tell me."

"So, it's going to look just like the Ponderosa,"

I begin, using my arms as I talk, so I drop my poles and trudge my way through the snow. "And it's going to sit back here in the trees. I want it to look like it's always been here, blending into the flora.

"I'm only going to knock down these trees that are already dead. The others stay, and it should give me plenty of space for the building. I'll reconfigure the inside a bit so there is a view of the lake from pretty much every room."

I prop my hands on my hips and take in the trees facing the water, weighed down with powder. I can see it so clearly in my head.

Now, I just have to make it a reality.

And I will.

"There are so few private residences in the park, Christian. It's rare, and it's a privilege to have this, to be able to share it with others. It's a magical place."

I turn back to him now and find him watching me with hungry eyes.

I can't read his expression.

"Well? What do you think?"

He looks back out to the water, and then the shoreline and the trees around me, then walks to me.

"I think it's amazing," he says. "I think *you're* amazing. And absolutely stunning as you talk about this passion of yours. You're so fierce, so determined, and I admire the hell out of you."

He takes my face in his hands and leans down to kiss me.

"You said earlier that you don't have a claim, and that my life isn't any of your business." His voice is hushed, the silence surrounds us, and it's as though we are truly the only two people in the world. "But you're wrong, Jenna. You do have a claim, and you have a say. I love you."

My breath catches in my throat. My God, did he just say what I think he did, or is the cold freezing my brain?

"For a thousand reasons, many of which I'm still learning, I love you. Your kindness, your passion for everything around you. You have quickly become the most important part of my life, and I'm so honored that you brought me here today, to share your dreams with me."

"It's important to me," I whisper, and gaze into his eyes. "And you're important to me."

"I don't know what's going to happen," he says honestly and tips his forehead against mine. "But I can tell you that I'm crazy about you, and I will be forever grateful that I met you, Jenna."

"I love you, too," I whisper and then tip my head back to take a long, deep breath before tackling us both into the soft snow. "You're a crazy man, you know that?"

"Crazy about you, fancy face," he says, then pins me down, kissing me silly. "I'm tempted to see if we can get this snow to melt."

"I refuse to get frostbite on my lady bits," I inform him, but I happily let him kiss the hell out of me some more.

Holy shit! Christian Wolfe just professed his love for me. I have so many questions, and the type-A side of me wants to drill him, make plans, figure it all out right now because I'm not one who loves surprises.

Well, the "I love you" was a good surprise.

But I'm going to take Natalie's advice, and I'm going to go with the flow. This is one thing in my life that I can't schedule the hell out of.

"I love this place," he whispers against my lips. "It's absolutely amazing, and I can't wait to see it when it's done."

That means he's planning to come back!

I'm full of hope and love. Desire.

"I can't wait to show you," I reply. "I hope I don't have issues with my contractors like I did last time, but we'll see."

"You'll handle it," he says, his voice strong with confidence. He stands and pulls me up to my feet. "Should we head back?"

"Yes. It'll start to get dark soon, and I promised you some hot tub sittin'."

"*Naked* hot tub sitting," he reminds me as we gather our poles and supplies. "And I'm collecting, sweetheart."

"I should hope so."

***

"So, what are you doing?" Max asks on the phone an hour later. I'd missed three texts and two calls from him, all of which came through once we found a cell signal, as there isn't one inside the park.

"We're driving back to town from the park property," I reply.

"Did you show Christian?"

"Yep."

"Are you heading home or up to the tree house?"

I frown and glance at Christian, who just shrugs as if to say *no clue.*

"I was going back up to the tree house, but do you need something?"

"Can you swing by my place?" he asks.

Max has a house on the lake, and it's on our way back to the tree house.

"Sure, I'll be there in about thirty minutes."

"See you soon."

I hang up and then shrug. "Sorry for the detour."

"No problem, the hot tub will still be there," Christian replies, takes my hand in his, pulls it up to his lips, and plants a wet kiss on my knuckles. "He sounded…concerned."

"He did," I agree, wondering what's up.

The roads into town are clear, so it doesn't take

long before we arrive at Max's house on the lake. His home is big, probably closer to what Christian is used to. And Max bought it for similar reasons.

Investment.

Because God knows that one man doesn't need a ten-thousand-square-foot house.

"Wow," Christian says with surprise. "I figured it would be nice, but this is *really* nice."

"He's wealthier than even you," I say and laugh when Christian narrows his eyes at me. "Well, he is. So, yeah. Investment."

"I get it," he says as he follows me to the grand front door that has an evergreen tree carved into it.

I don't even have time to ring the bell when Max opens the door. His dark hair is disheveled. He's in sweats and a ratty old sweatshirt.

"You look like shit," I say as I walk into his house, shed my coat, and hang it on a hook by the door.

"Thanks," he says grimly and leads us into his kitchen.

"I'm sorry to intrude," Christian begins, but Max waves him off.

"You're not. It's cool."

"What's wrong?"

"I'll show you," he says and gestures for us to follow him down to the basement.

I can smell it halfway down.

"Well, shit."

Max laughs humorlessly. "Not funny."

"Your sewer is backed up. Did you call someone?"

"Yeah, I called you."

I sigh and glance back at Christian. "We're going back upstairs. This is disgusting."

"You can't leave," Max says, and I just laugh.

"I'm not leaving, I'm going to make some calls where it doesn't smell like I'm swimming in a sewer."

I settle at Max's massive kitchen island and make my way through my phone.

"No one is open on Sunday," I murmur, then remember that a friend of mine owes me a favor. "Wait. I know someone."

Five minutes later, I have Fred on his way over to take a look.

"I pretty much just saved the day. But why didn't you just make some calls? Rather than to me?"

"I didn't know who to call," he says with a scowl. "You're the one who does the construction stuff. I design software."

"And run an empire," I add, then lean in and kiss his cheek. "Fred will fix it."

"Thank God. It's fucking gross." He glances over to Christian. "What did you think of the park property?"

"It's ridiculous," Christian says, shaking his head. "I've never seen anything like it."

"It'll be better once she works her magic on it." He points his thumb at me and then winks. "She's good for something."

"I'm good for lots of things, I'll have you know." I push my nose into the air like I'm offended and march in the direction of my coat. "Now, we're going up to the tree house where we plan to spend some naked time in the hot tub."

"That's way more information than I ever need."

"You deserved it."

CHAPTER THIRTEEN

Jenna

"YOU GUYS LOOK AMAZING," I say the following evening as the girls and I sip wine and open our presents to each other.

"I love the tiaras you got us," Willa says with a giggle, touching the pretty crown on her head.

"A girl needs a tiara," I reply with a shrug. "Besides, I'm running out of ideas on what to get you guys. We already have *everything*."

"I feel very royal," Grace says, her face sober as she gives us all a stoic wave, pretending to greet her subjects.

"Isn't Jacob a royal?" I ask and reach for a box of Milk Duds. We've decided to have movie night in Grace and Jacob's home theater, so we have all of the movie essentials; candy, popcorn, soda, and possible diabetes.

"He's a cousin of somebody or other," she says

with a frown. "I don't think he has an official title."

"Well, I'd say we all made out like bandits," Hannah says as she slips the scarf Willa got her around her neck. "And I'm just grateful that y'all include me."

Our circle isn't big, but it's tight.

"What do you think of *my* present?" Willa asks while hiding a laugh behind her hand, and I glance over at the life-sized cutout of Christian Wolfe sitting next to me. He's in a tux, but the tie is undone, along with his shirt. We can see his spectacular chest and abs.

It's actually kind of hot.

And funny as hell.

"He's hot," Grace says with a sigh. "No disrespect intended."

I laugh and drag my hand down his flat, cold stomach. "It's better doing this in person."

"Now you're just bragging," Grace replies, making us all laugh.

"Is he nice to you?" Hannah asks as she pours popcorn kernels in the old-fashioned popper of Grace's.

"Of course, he is. I wouldn't have talked to him after that first conversation if he was a dick. He'd be on his own."

"And the sex," Willa says, pushing her long, dark hair over her shoulder. "On a scale of meh to what the fuck was that?"

I bust out laughing and throw a Milk Dud at her, but she isn't deterred.

"Seriously," Hannah says. "We need to know."

"So, you know the man can dance," I begin, and they all nod, staring at me as if I'm about to tell them the secrets of the universe.

And maybe I am. The girl secrets, anyway.

"He can move his body in ways that just defy comprehension. And I'm not talking about being flexible or weird here. Like, he constantly hears a beat in his head and he moves with it *all the time.* Whether he's walking or cooking or making love to me, it's just effortless."

"Wow," Grace breathes, rubbing her round belly. "That made the baby kick."

"And I won't deny that he's hot. I mean, look at him."

"I have to interject here and just say," Willa says, "that the two of you together is just ridiculously beautiful. It's kind of not fair to those of us who are just average-looking."

"Shut up." I roll my eyes, but they all nod their heads in unison.

"I know you don't love that people only see your face," Willa adds. "And you know that's not all we see. We love you, inside and out. But I just want to remind you that he's not the only hot one in this relationship."

I eat a Dud and ponder what she's saying. "I

appreciate that. You're sweet."

"I can't wait to see you walk a red carpet together," Grace says and gives an excited dance.

"There are no plans for that." I grimace and set my Milk Duds aside.

"Are there plans at all?" Hannah asks.

"The plan is to enjoy him for the next twelve or so days, and then we'll see. But we said the *L* word yesterday."

"*What?*" Grace screeches, then flings her arms around me and hugs me tight. "Oh my God, that's so great."

Willa holds my gaze from across the room and sips her wine. She looks happy for me and apprehensive at the same time.

And I get it. So, I offer her a small shrug.

"Now, we have one more surprise for you," Hannah says as she begins to hand out fresh popcorn to the three of us. "We're doing movie night like we said."

"But it's all Christian Wolfe movies," Grace says with a laugh as we walk into the theater. There are ten massive leather recliners and two loveseats in front of a giant screen. Vintage movie posters line the walls.

"Christian would love this room," I murmur as I take a seat in the middle row, settling in with my goodies.

"He's here," Willa says, stationing the cardboard cutout at the end of my row, facing me.

"Why does he have to watch me? It's creepy."

"Good point." She turns him so he's facing the screen. "There. Now he can watch the movie, too."

Grace gets the movie queued up, the lights dim, and soon, Christian comes on the screen, working a crime scene.

His hair is darker in this role. He's clean-shaven like he was the day he arrived not that long ago. He's since let his stubble grow.

I like it both ways.

There's action, suspense, and even some romance.

"Oh, boy, look away," Hannah says, shoveling popcorn into her mouth. "Your man's gonna kiss that floozy."

"We're rooting for her," I remind her with a laugh.

But then his lips are on her, his hands gripping her shoulders the way he sometimes grips mine, and I tip my head to the side, studying it.

It's just a kiss between two fictional characters. No big deal. They're interrupted by something sinister, and the movie progresses with more action.

About an hour later, the mood of the film changes, and it becomes much sexier.

Like, get naked and roll around sexy.

And I don't love it.

"Uh-oh," Willa says, watching me. "She doesn't like this part."

"I was okay with the kissing," I admit, and have to look away when I can see his fully naked backside covering her supposedly naked body, and he's moving as if he's inside her. "But, no. I don't like the sex."

"It's not real sex," Hannah says, then swallows hard. "Although, he's a good actor. It looks pretty real."

"There are dozens of people watching," Grace reminds us.

Thankfully, it's over quickly. The movie ends shortly after, and the lights come up.

"Are you okay?" Willa asks.

"Of course," I reply. "It's a movie. It isn't real."

"One more," Grace says. "And this one is a comedy, and if I remember correctly, Christian doesn't take his clothes off. Much to my dismay."

"Let's do it."

Halfway into this movie, Christian asks a woman to marry him. Is it sweet and fun? Yes. Is it also a bit weird?

Sort of, yes.

His hair is much blonder in this film, and he's got his scruff going on. The actress is cute and quirky, and when he asks her to marry him, she clutches her heart and starts to cry.

"I want the have-you-seen-the-way-he-looks-at-her kind of love," Willa says with a sigh. "I think I'm there, you guys. It's been years, and I miss being part of a *we*."

She has that, she's just too damn blind to see it. My brother is a wreck every time he looks at her.

I wish they weren't both so stubborn.

***

"Where are we going?" I ask Christian the following afternoon.

"It's a surprise."

I smile and lean in to kiss his cheek. "I like your surprises, but I need to know *something* so I can dress accordingly."

His eyes skim over my mostly naked body.

"Maybe we should skip it and stay here," he suggests, his hand gliding over my ass.

"No way. You promised me a surprise."

He laughs. "Okay. Dress warm."

"Are we going outside?"

He nods, and I can tell I won't get much more information out of him, so I pull on some jeans, a long-sleeved T-shirt, and a red flannel.

"You know, it's that time of year when most women look cute in their flannels. I look like I've misplaced my ax."

He lets out a surprised laugh and wraps his arms around me from behind. "Stop it. You're beautiful."

"I can't wait for summer," I murmur. "Okay. I'm about ready. Am I driving?"

"No, ma'am. I'm driving."

"Do you know where you're going?"

He frowns, pretending to look hurt. "How could you question my natural sense of direction?"

"Come on, then, I want to see what the surprise is."

We walk out of his tree house and down to his rental SUV, which is already running.

"Fancy," I comment, wiggling my eyebrows.

"It has an app, so my lady doesn't have to get into a cold vehicle." He opens my door for me, then shuts it when I'm inside and settled.

He drives us down toward town. The roads are treacherous today after a heavy snowfall last night and today.

"They plowed, but it's icy," I murmur. "Are you sure you're okay to drive?"

"I'm sure," he says. He has both hands on the wheel and he's watching the road carefully. "I have precious cargo with me, and I'm a trained driver."

I'm quiet as he works his way down the mountain, silently holding my breath and praying that we don't slide.

Am I a bit of a control freak?

Maybe.

But we reach the bottom safely, and he turns

toward town.

"You can breathe now," he says and tosses me a wink.

"It's not that I don't trust your driving skills. It's just that you're from L.A. and you don't drive in snow and ice very often."

"Or ever," he agrees with a nod and pats my leg. "But I won't take chances or get cocky."

Once in town, he drives past downtown and behind the post office where there's a pond. Every winter, the city makes it an ice skating rink, and I immediately know what we're about to do.

"Ice skating?"

He smiles excitedly as he parks, throws it out of gear, and hurries around to my side to help me out of the SUV.

We are the only car here. Someone strung lights between the trees above the pond, and as the sun is setting, it casts a soft glow over the space.

It's dreamy.

He takes my hand and leads me to the edge of the pond where there's a blanket laid over the snowbank. Two pairs of skates are set out for us, along with a thermos and a cooler.

"Where is everyone else?"

"I rented it out for the evening," he says nonchalantly as he leans on the snowbank and trades his boots for skates. "Come on, I'll help you."

I lean on the blanket, and he gets to work trading my boots for the skates, then puts his gloves back on, stands, and holds out a hand for me.

"So, I have a confession," I say, looking around at the empty rink, the lights overhead, and everything that he had done for me.

"What's that?"

"I can't dance. I can't find rhythm, and it's not easy for me."

He shakes his head, but I hold up my hand, stopping him so I can continue.

"But I can *skate*." And with that, I push off of the snowbank and set off across the ice, loving the cold against my cheeks, and the smell of the snow as it falls lightly around me.

Christian catches up with me, wraps his arms around me, and we skate together, turning and laughing.

Laughing *so hard*.

"I didn't expect this," he says, his painfully handsome face lit up. "You're amazing on skates."

"Winters are long in Montana," I remind him and then spin around. "We played on this ice all the time growing up. It's been a couple of years."

"It looks like you were born on it," he replies.

"How are you so good at it?"

He just laughs and skates away from me, back to the blanket. He fiddles with something, and the next thing I know, there's music in the air.

"Where are the speakers?"

He returns to me and pulls me against him, front to front. Our breath is coming fast and in soft puffs of air around us, and he's gazing down at me in that way that Willa was talking about last night.

And you know what I realize? He never looked at those other women in the movies like this. He's an excellent actor, but he didn't look at them as if they hung the stars.

"Are you okay?" he asks.

"How did you do all of this?"

His gaze flicks down to my lips, then back to my eyes. "Brad helped."

"I always liked him best."

He smiles and pulls me into a slow dance around the ice.

"You're good at this, too."

"Athletic things have always come naturally to me," he admits as he leads me around the ice. "I'm not afraid of it. I know I can do it."

"What are you afraid of?"

He blinks rapidly, his eyebrows pulling together slightly as he stares down at me.

"Honestly, not much. But I'm afraid of losing this, with you. Of leaving here and never having a moment like this with you again."

Tears threaten as I press my fingers to his lips.

"We have it now," I whisper. "And it's so good,

Christian. You're not going to lose me after you leave. We will figure something out."

He kisses me fiercely, then takes my hand, and we skate around the pond as fast as we can. It's thrilling, exciting. And after the third time around, we return to the blanket.

"I have hot chocolate," he says, breathing hard. "And we have some hot soup and sandwiches, too."

"Oh my God, this is amazing." I sit on the snowbank, and he passes me the goodies. "Thank you. This might be the best date I've ever been on."

"Then my work here is done."

He bows deeply, then takes a bite of a sandwich. I've never been treated so...*well.* And that's not to say that I've been treated poorly in the past. It's just that no other man has even come *close* to making me feel as pampered, as important as Christian has done in just the past thirty minutes.

Trust me when I say the city doesn't pay for twinkling lights and speaker systems at this little ice rink. No, this is something Christian had done, just for this date.

And he had it catered.

"How did you know my shoe size?"

"I looked at your shoes," he says. "And I have a confession of my own."

"Oh, good, I can't wait to hear this."

He laughs and takes another bite of his sandwich. "I have a shoe fetish."

I stop chewing and stare at him, then work on swallowing my food. "If you tell me that you want to lick my shoes while we fuck, we're going to need to have a serious conversation. Because while I'm all for everyone having all the safe and consensual sex they want to, I'm not into anyone licking my shoes. That's just not sanitary."

He's laughing, squatting in his skates because he can't stand anymore from the laughter.

"No," he cries out when he can breathe again. "I don't want to lick your shoes. I might lick your *feet,* though."

"That's different altogether."

"But I wouldn't mind if you *wore* the shoes sometime when we're making love."

I sip my hot chocolate. "My snow boots aren't very sexy."

His lips twitch. "I've seen some pretty heels in your closet."

"True, I do have some pretty heels. I usually only get to wear them in the summer, and it's a treat. I like shoes, too."

"All I'm saying is, if you should want to wear said shoes in the *winter*, now you have a reason."

"It's a pretty good reason." A vision of Christian holding onto the heels of my shoes as he fucks me from behind enters my head, and I smile slowly.

Yes, it's a good reason indeed.

"Keep thinking like that, and you'll melt that

snowbank," he says conversationally as he packs up what's left of our dinner. "Are you ready to go?"

"Absolutely not." I push off and skate across the pond again. Now that I've had some rest, I'm ready to go. This is excellent exercise. I can feel it in my ass already.

I'll be sore tomorrow.

But it's so worth it.

Halfway Gone by Lifehouse fills the air, and Christian catches up to me, pulls me against him, and we dance across the ice.

I wish someone were here to film *this*. Having these moments caught on film would be priceless.

But he made it clear early on that he doesn't like photos.

"What are you thinking?" he asks.

"I'd like a photo of this." I kiss his chin. "But it's okay."

He scowls. "We can absolutely have a photo," he replies and pulls his phone out of his pocket, then holds it out to take a selfie. I tip my forehead against his cheek and smile, and he captures the moment.

"Thank you."

"Here, I have a better idea."

He skates to the side of the pond and sets his phone in the snow, facing me. He fiddles with his watch and skates back to me, looking down.

"I'm going to press record, and we'll skate a bit."

"A video?" I do a little bounce, and he bites his lip, watching me.

"Absolutely. Let's do it."

He presses the button, then pulls me into his arms, and we float around the ice. He spins me and actually gets me to dance a bit.

It's the most fun I've had in *years*.

When the song ends, he dips me back and kisses me soundly, then pushes my hat higher up on my forehead.

"I love you, fancy face."

"I love you, too."

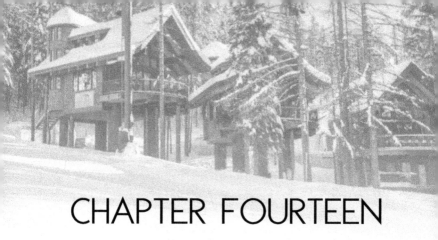

CHAPTER FOURTEEN

Jenna

"I'M COLD," I SAY as we climb the steps to the tree house. The other two units are still empty until tomorrow when I'll greet two new groups of guests.

In the meantime, Christian and I are all alone.

"Hot tub," he says immediately, making me grin. "Hey, we never got around to it the other night."

"If I recall correctly, you dragged me into the bedroom, stripped me bare, and wouldn't let me leave the bed for the next twelve hours."

"A man has priorities," he says with a shrug, pulling his coat off and then mine and hanging them on the hall tree by the front door. "And a sexy woman to take care of."

"You're sweet." I tuck my hands under my arms, willing them to warm up. "I think I skated for too long. It was just so *fun*! I didn't want to leave."

"We can always go back," he says with a laugh and leads me to the living area. "Here, sit down, and I'll go get the tub ready."

"Oh, there's a lock, and you have to—"

"I know my way around a hot tub," he assures me and disappears outside. The snow is still falling harder up here on the mountain. It's pretty, but it's also coming to that time of year when I just long for spring.

Christian walks back inside and crooks a finger at me. "Come here."

"Yes, sir, bossy man." I stand and walk to him. He gets to work stripping me naked, then lifts me in his arms and carries me out to the tub. "Oh, shit, it's cold."

"Not for long." He lowers me down into the water, and I immediately sigh in happiness. "You soak for a few. I'll be back."

He shuts the door behind him, and I'm left outside, watching the snow fall and letting the hot water soak into my skin.

When Christian returns, he's carrying towels and two glasses of wine, and if I weren't already in love with him, I would fall all over again.

"Here you go," he says, passing me both glasses so he can set the towels aside.

He's blissfully naked. His muscles move with ease, and it's as though the cold doesn't bother him at all as he moves about the deck.

He finally swings a leg over and joins me. I pass him his glass and take a sip of mine, watching him over the rim.

"Thanks for this evening," I say.

"I had fun, too," he says. "God, that snow is beautiful."

"Hmm." I watch it for a while in silence as we enjoy our wine and our soak. "I love it until about the middle of January."

"What happens then?"

"Well, I love the change of seasons, and when the snow starts, it ramps up for Christmas, and I love the holidays. But after New Year's, it's just snow. Months and months of snow."

"You get sick of it."

"I do. February is the longest month of the year here, and if we're lucky, we start to melt out around the end of March."

"You should spend February somewhere warm," he suggests, and I nod, considering.

"I would, but I have businesses to run here."

"Could you hire an agency to take care of the rentals while you're gone?"

I smile and sip my wine. "A type-A control freak has issues with such things."

"You're not a control freak."

"I am when it comes to my business. But to

answer your question, yes. I could. In theory. But I'm not the wealthy sibling. That's Max. Although, he does own a nice condo near San Diego that he hardly uses."

I glance over at Christian and grimace.

"Sorry, I'm babbling."

"No, you're thinking out loud." He swirls his wine, watching it. "I could take you somewhere warm. Anywhere you want to go."

"I wasn't fishing around for a vacation offer from you, Christian."

He sloshes through the water, sets our wine glasses aside, and scoops me into his lap. My shoulders are out of the hot water and in the cool air, and his eyes are hot on me.

He looks almost frustrated.

"I don't know how much to offer or what to say," he says and cups my cheek in his wet hand. "So, I'm just going to say what I'm thinking. Accepting gifts from me doesn't make you a gold digger."

"I didn't say—"

"Let me finish."

I swallow my words and close my mouth.

"I have more money than I can ever spend in my lifetime, Jenna. I'm not bragging, it's just fact. I could buy you a fucking island if that's what you want."

"I don't really need a whole island."

He covers my lips with his finger.

"Shh." I bite his fingertip, and he keeps talking. "All I'm suggesting is, if you'd like to leave for the month of February to get out of the snow for a while, we can make that happen."

I push my fingers through his hair, wetting it.

"You're not saying anything."

"You told me to shut it."

He laughs and lifts my hips, then settles me over his hard cock and slides easily into me.

"You were such a plot twist," he murmurs against my lips before kissing me silly. I don't even care that I'm partially out of the water, all I can feel is Christian. Under me and inside me, he's all I can focus on. "You make me lose my mind."

I move over him, rocking my hips and making the water sluice over our bodies, over the side of the tub. His lips lock on my breast, his hands cupping my ass.

I lean in and press my forehead to his, and the next thing I know, I'm sitting on the edge of the tub, and he's standing in the water, fucking me hard and fast.

The combination of cold air, hot water, and the sexiest man I know doing unspeakably insane things to my body is almost too much for me to handle.

I combust, exploding into a million stars, and when I come back together again, Christian is there, holding me and smiling at me.

He lowers us back into the water, and I slip back onto his lap to lay my head on his shoulder.

"I had no idea that vacation talk did that to you," I say, earning a kiss on the forehead.

"*You* do that to me."

***

"Here." I hold a frozen huckleberry to Christian's lips the next morning. He plucks it out of my fingers with his lips and then kisses my fingertips.

"Mm." He grabs one of my ponytails and gives it a tug. "You look young with these."

"I just wanted my hair out of my way," I reply and get back to work making huckleberry pancakes. "Do you have the movie ready?"

"Yes, ma'am," he says and leans against the countertop, drinking out of my mug that has a picture of a taco and says *Every now and then I fall apart*. "Are you sure you want to watch that movie?"

"Why? You said I could pick the first one."

I flip the pancakes and glance his way. He's shirtless again, which doesn't hurt my feelings in the least. How is it that it's December and he's been here for almost three weeks, and he still looks tan?

It's ridiculous.

"I know, I'm just making sure *this* is the movie you want to watch."

I frown. "What's wrong with *Steel Magnolias*?"

His brows climb on his forehead, and then he takes another sip of coffee.

"It has really good actors in it," I remind him.

"You're right."

"And it's one of my favorites." I put the pancakes in the oven to keep warm, then pour two more onto the skillet. "Do you hate it or something?"

"I don't get it," he finally admits. "I just don't think it's about *anything*. Except sadness and despair."

I bust out laughing. "It's about friendship, Christian."

"People die and have surgeries and weddings. And a baby."

"Yes." I sprinkle huckleberries on the pancakes. "See, you just need a refresher so you can finally see the genius of the film."

He sets his mug down and wraps his arms around me from behind, pressing his already semi-hard cock against my lower back.

"What do I have to do to talk you into something else?"

"If you hate it that much, I'll pick a different one."

I flip the pancakes, and he spins me around, cupping my face and kissing me senseless. "You'd do that for me?" he asks against my lips.

"I mean, it's a hardship, but yes. I don't want to torture you."

He grins. "You'd better take those pancakes off the burner."

"Oh!" I turn and pull them off just in time, but before I can make more, he slides the skillet off the flame and tugs me back into his arms. "Christian, I'm trying to cook you breakfast here."

"And I need to show you my appreciation." He nuzzles my neck and slides his hands under my pajama pants, cupping my bare ass. "You're not wearing panties."

"You just take them off."

He moans in agreement and works the elastic down my hips, and the pants pool around my ankles.

"Cooking while naked isn't safe," I remind him.

"It's a good thing you're not cooking anymore." He boosts me onto the countertop and squats, eye level with my pussy. "Look at you, all wet and ready for me."

"I mean, you kissed my neck, so it's not really my fault."

"I'm going to kiss more than your neck."

Never one to make hollow promises, he buries his face in my core and takes me on a rollercoaster ride of sensation, from light interest to burning orgasm in about six seconds.

Jesus, the man is good with his mouth.

He stands and is tall enough to sink inside me, right there, bracing himself against the cupboards as he moves in and out.

My shirt's still on, but he pushes the hem up so he can cup my breast, teasing the nipple in his fingertips.

"You fucking turn me on," he growls just before he comes spectacularly, leans in to kiss me, and then helps me off the counter. "I think it's your smart mouth."

"I am rather smart," I agree as I shimmy back into my pants and finish making breakfast. "Now, if I let you eat this in bed, you have to promise not to get crumbs in the sheets." I turn to look at him, take in the sexiness, and reconsider. "Actually, I wouldn't kick you out of bed unless you wanted to do it on the floor."

He snickers as he carries the syrup, butter, and our forks to the bed. *Steel Magnolias* is queued up on the TV.

"We can change it."

"What would you rather watch?"

I think about it for a moment, buttering my pancakes. "*Beaches*," I reply, and he flops back on the bed, covering his face with a pillow and yelling as if he's in great pain.

I can't help but laugh at him as he peeks out at me.

"You're killing me, fancy face."

"It's a classic."

"It's *sad*. Why do girls always want to watch sad movies?"

"Okay, let me think." I take a bite of my pancakes, then reach for a piece of bacon. "I haven't seen that one with Matt Damon where he gets stuck on Mars."

"That's one I can get behind," he says and reaches for the remote.

"Have you seen it?"

"I've seen almost everything," he replies. "And I don't mind watching it again."

"Is it like doing homework? I watch a lot of HGTV, and I go on the Parade of Homes and stuff because I like seeing what's out there in real estate. Is it the same with you and movies?"

He takes a bite of bacon, thinking it over. "Sort of, I guess. But mostly, I just love films. I enjoy being swept up in the fiction of it."

"Fairy tales are a fun place to be swept up in."

"I think that's why, although I can respect the acting in movies like *Steel Magnolias* and *Beaches*, they aren't my favorites. It's not that I don't want to be moved, to feel what they're feeling. But I don't like it when there's not a happily ever after. That's what Hollywood is all about, in my opinion."

"You want it all to work out in the end."

"Absolutely. I want to leave the theater with

hope. I don't want to be sad for the rest of the day."

"I can see that." I finish my breakfast and set my plate on the floor. "Did I tell you that the girls and I watched a couple of your films the other night?"

He stops chewing and narrows his eyes at me. "No. You didn't."

"Well, we did."

"Which ones?"

I tell him, and he smiles. "Who picked?"

"Grace, I think. She and Jacob have an amazing theater in their house."

"I have one in my house in L.A., as well. It's my favorite room in the place."

I frown, reminded that he has a big life in California that doesn't have much of anything to do with me.

But I refuse to let it interfere with my time with Christian while he's here in Cunningham Falls.

"What did you think of them?"

"I'd seen one before. I hadn't seen the other and didn't realize that you got naked in it."

He shrugs. "And?"

"It was…uncomfortable." I bite my lip, thinking about how I felt watching him seemingly make love to someone else. "You're a good actor, I'll give you that."

"So, let me tell you what really goes down in those scenes," he says and sets his own empty plate on the floor. "There were sixteen people in the room. Yes, I counted. It was cold, and I asked them to turn up the heat, but the soundstage we were on was just drafty, and there wasn't much they could do about it.

"So, Krista, my co-star, was also naked and not entirely comfortable with it."

"Why?"

"This was the day after we'd met for the first time," he replies. "We didn't know each other well, and she's actually kind of shy. So, I was doing my best to keep her covered and hidden from the crew. Between takes, I'd reach for a blanket and throw it over her while the crew made adjustments and stuff."

"Not exactly romantic."

He takes my hand and kisses my knuckles. "No. Not to mention, she's married in real life with three kids. One of her kids had the flu, and she was worried about her, but you'd never know it from her performance. She is a professional, through and through."

"You like her."

"I do." He falls back against the pillows, crossing his arms behind his head. His biceps flex, making my mouth water. "I respect her as an actor and as a person. She's nice. So, anyway, that scene took two days to shoot, and it wasn't even an eighth as sexy as they made it look in the movie."

"Interesting."

"If you ever want to, you're welcome to come to the set and watch."

I sigh, rub my hands over my face, then stand and gather our plates and take them out to the kitchen and walk back again, trying to pull my thoughts together. I lean on the doorjamb, watching him. He hasn't moved.

"I don't think there will ever come a day that I'll ask to go with you on set to watch you pretend that you're fucking another woman."

He starts to speak, but I hold up my hand.

"I know it's not real. And I'm not calling it cheating or wrong or anything like that. It's fiction, and it's part of your job. But I don't want to watch it in live action."

"Come here."

I climb back onto the bed, but before I can snuggle up next to him, he pins me to the mattress and pulls the covers over us completely as if we're in a blanket fort.

"It *is* my job," he says softly as his eyes travel over my face. "And I love my job. But I don't love it more than you."

"Christian—"

"Shh." He kisses me, then bites my lower lip. "It's my turn to talk now. You're welcome to come and watch whatever you want. I'll never hide anything. And if you don't want to, that's okay, too."

"Thank you."

"But the kissing in roles, and sometimes the racier scenes will happen."

"I know."

"Are you okay?" He brushes his nose against mine in that way he does that makes my knees weak.

"Yes."

"You need to know," he begins as he kisses my neck, reawakening my body in all the right places, "that when I'm doing my job, I don't feel like *this*." He presses his hard-on against my inner thigh. "And I don't look at my co-stars the way I look at you."

"I know that, too," I reply and cup his face in my hands. "I thought of that last night when we were skating. Because I won't lie, I didn't love watching you with other women on-screen. But then, when we were skating, it occurred to me that the look on your face in the movie wasn't even close to the same as when you're looking at *me*. And that's really all I need to know, Christian."

"You take my breath away," he whispers and sinks into me. Where the kitchen was playful and even a bit frantic, this is slow. Private. Loving and sensual.

And damn it, I can't get enough of him.

I never want this to end.

CHAPTER FIFTEEN

Christian

"ICAN'T BELIEVE YOU'RE craving ice cream in the middle of a blizzard," I say as I maneuver my rented SUV down the mountain. Jenna smirks at me in that way she does that makes me want to pull the car over, yank her into my lap, and kiss the fuck out of her.

"This isn't a blizzard, city boy," she says. "This is snow."

"*Cold* snow," I remind her. "And now you want *ice* cream."

"The cravings for ice cream don't stop with the seasons," she says reasonably and shifts in her seat to face me. "Are you telling me that in the summer in L.A. you stop eating hot food?"

I send her the side-eye. She has a point.

And she knows it because she tips her head back and giggles.

"Okay, which grocery store are we going to?"

"Why in the world would we go to the grocery store?"

"For ice cream."

She shakes her head. "No way. We're going to Sweet Scoops. They have the *best* handmade ice cream. Seriously, it's going to change your life."

"That's a bold statement." I glance over at her to laugh, and just that fast, an elk the size of Manhattan runs out in front of us. The next three seconds happen in slow motion.

I press on the brake as Jenna grips onto the dash. I spin the wheel frantically to the left where the ditch and the mountain is. There's a dropoff on the right, and we do *not* want to go that way.

But rather than go into the ditch peacefully, the SUV spins, catching on black ice, and we go out of control.

My heart is in my throat, racing.

Jenna is screaming.

The front end of the SUV slams into the snowbank, and our airbags immediately go off.

I don't lose consciousness. I push the bag out of my way.

"Jenna! Baby, are you okay?"

No answer. She's leaning back, blood coming from somewhere on her head, and she's unconscious.

Christ, what if I've killed her?

I check her pulse. It's strong and fast in her neck, and I send a prayer of thanks as I dial 911.

"What is your emergency?"

"Car accident," I say immediately, shocked at how confident my voice sounds. "I'm okay, but my girlfriend is unconscious."

"Where are you?"

I relay the information the best I can, frustrated that I don't know the name of the road we're on. But the dispatcher seems to know and assures me that an ambulance will be here in less than ten minutes.

"The faster, the better."

I hang up and jump out of the car, then hurry to the other side where Jenna is and jerk the door open to better see if she has other injuries.

"Christian?" she asks, her voice thin.

"Yes, baby, I'm here."

"Did we hit the elk?"

"No, we hit a snowbank." I swallow hard and kiss her cheek. "The ambulance is on the way."

"I don't feel so good," she says and reaches up to touch her head. "Bleeding."

"You have a small cut on your head." I swallow again, not sure if that was my first lie to her or not. I can't see the cut, but I can see the damn blood. "Do you hurt anywhere else?"

Sirens finally fill the air. They're still a ways away, but they're getting closer.

"I don't think so," she says with a frown. "I'm sleepy."

"Don't go back to sleep. The EMTs are going to need to ask you questions."

"Don't care."

"Jenna, baby, do *not* go to sleep. Look at me."

She complies, and I see that her eyes are both dilated. I'm not a doctor. I don't even play one on TV. But even I know that isn't a good sign.

Finally, the ambulance and a fire truck pull up behind my vehicle, and the EMTs come out.

"Thank God, she's over here," I call out.

"Is she conscious?" one of them asks.

"She is now, but she says she's tired."

"I'm Sam, and we're going to take care of your girl," he assures me, then looks into the car. "Hey, Jenna."

He sticks his head out of the vehicle and yells over my shoulder. "This is Jenna Hull, guys. Call the chief!"

"Don't freak Brad out, I'm fine," I hear her say, but Sam shakes his head.

"No can do, pretty girl. Your brother would kill me if I didn't let him know that you're hurt. Besides, he probably already heard about the call."

Another man appears with a gurney. They pull

Jenna out of the car, secure her neck with a brace, and strap her onto the stretcher.

"Come on, sir," Sam says, waving at me. "You can ride with us."

"Wild horses and all the paparazzi in the world couldn't keep me away," I mutter as I retrieve Jenna's bag and slam the SUV door closed. I climb into the back of the ambulance and take Jenna's hand. "Hey, baby."

"Hi," she says, watching me with scared, blue eyes. "Have I mentioned that I don't like being tied down? I have some claustrophobia issues."

"Can you untie her?"

"I can untie her arms, sure, but her neck has to stay stabilized until a doctor can examine her and make sure she doesn't have a broken neck."

"I don't," Jenna says.

"Sorry, Jen, but here…you can move your arms around."

He unfastens her arms, and she sighs. "That's a little better."

The ride to the hospital takes less than ten minutes. Once we're there, they rush her back into a room and let me follow. I stand back while the staff does their thing, talking loudly, moving her to a bed, starting an IV, and asking her a ton of questions.

Her eyes seem heavy, but she keeps looking for me. I smile reassuringly, but all the while, my stomach is in knots, and pure adrenaline runs through me.

I want to punch someone as hard as I can.

She could have *died* on that mountain, and it would have been my fucking fault.

Soon after we arrive, they wheel Jenna out for a CT scan of her head and neck, and I'm left in the room alone.

Until Brad and Max walk in.

"Jesus," I mutter and push my hands through my hair. "I'm glad to see you guys. I don't think I've ever been so fucking scared."

"Is she okay?" Max asks.

"They took her back for a CT scan," I reply. "That airbag hit her hard. I would be surprised if she doesn't have a concussion, but I'm not a doctor."

"What happened?" Brad asks. His face is taut with worry, his voice is hard.

"Fucking elk ran out in front of us coming down the mountain."

"Thank God you went into the ditch and not down the dropoff," Max says, rubbing his forehead.

"We hit ice and spun out. Hit the ditch and the snowbank."

"Could have been much worse," Brad says, agreeing with Max. "That mountain road can be a bitch in the winter."

Finally, Jenna is wheeled back in, looking tired but still awake.

"Oh, good," she says. "My three favorite guys are here. You can tell them," she says to the doctor.

"Jenna has a concussion," he says. "But no broken bones. She'll be sore and maybe a little black and blue."

The doctor glances at me, and his eyes narrow. "You were the driver?"

I take Jenna's hand in mine and nod.

"Have you been checked out?" he asks.

"I'm fine," I insist. "We need to take care of Jenna."

"You need to get checked, too, Christian," Jenna says and squeezes my hand. "I'll be okay. I have two brothers here to watch over things."

"Come with me," the doctor says, but I hang back with uncertainty.

"We'll come get you if anything happens," Brad assures me. "But she's fine."

I nod. "Thanks, man. I'll be right back."

I'm led to a small room not far from Jenna's.

"Put this gown on—"

"Fuck that. Just look me over, take my blood pressure, and let me get back to Jenna."

The doctor scowls. "Just because you're famous—"

"Oh, for godsake, I don't give a shit about my

job. I need to get back to my girl. I don't have any pain."

"Yet," he says but starts looking me over, poking and prodding. He takes my temperature and checks my blood pressure. "That's up a bit, but I'd expect that after the trauma. I don't see anything concerning but listen to your body over the next couple of days and take it easy."

I nod and stand. "Thanks. Can I please go back now?"

"I don't think I could stop you."

I hurry back and stop at the doorway, taking in the scene before me.

Max is sitting next to Jenna, holding her hand and making her smile. Brad is standing on the other side of her, talking on the phone.

"She's going to be okay," he says. "They'll spring her out of here soon. I'm sure Christian will stay with her."

"Damn right, he will."

All three pairs of eyes turn to me. Jenna's light up in happiness, and she holds out her free hand for me. Brad steps out into the hall to finish his call, and I take her hand, kiss it, and then sit on the bed near her hip.

"How do you feel, fancy face?"

"Like my face isn't so fancy," she replies.

"It's not," Max says, making her giggle.

"Don't make me laugh, idiot. It hurts."

"I'm sorry," he says. "You know I have a bad sense of humor when I'm scared."

"You're not scared of anything," she says. She pulls her hand out of his and cups his cheek. "You're the fiercest person I know."

"No," he replies, kissing her hand. "That's *you*."

Brad returns. "Hannah's in the middle of delivering a baby so she can't come see you herself, but she said she'd look in on you later."

"She's sweet," Jenna replies. "But I swear I'm okay. Do I get to sleep?"

"It says here," I reply as I'm reading the material the doctor gave me, "that you can sleep, but I have to wake you every couple of hours."

"Lovely," she says.

"Glad it's not me," Brad says with a laugh. "She's a bear when you wake her up."

"I'm not afraid of bears," I reply.

"You should be."

*****

It's a couple of hours later by the time Max delivers us to Jenna's house in town. He hurries in ahead of us and flips on the lights and turns on the gas fireplace.

I carry Jenna in my arms into the house. She's curled against my chest, her head tucked under my chin.

"Do you want to snuggle up on the couch?" I ask her.

"I think I need a shower," she says, her voice still quiet. "And then bed."

"Do you need me for anything else?" Max asks.

"Right now, no, but we'll need her car brought down at some point. Could you help with that?"

"Sure thing, I'll have Brad help me with that first thing in the morning." He brushes her hair off of her cheek and leans in to press a kiss there. "Get some rest, and I'll see you tomorrow."

"Thanks, Max," she says.

He nods and leaves, and I carry my girl to her master suite and set her gently on the edge of her bed.

"Can you sit here while I get the shower ready?"

"I think so."

She looks so small and fragile, and I feel like absolute shit. It's because of *me* that she's hurting.

I'd gladly change places with her if I could. I hate that this happened.

I get the hot water going and set out a fresh towel and washcloth. When I come back to the bedroom, she's struggling to get her shirt off, then stops in frustration.

"This is ridiculous," she mutters. "How does taking off my shirt make me so tired?"

"Your brain is hurt, honey," I remind her and

get to work gently removing her clothes. My breath hisses between my teeth when I see the bruises on her chest from the seatbelt. "Oh, baby. I'm so sorry."

"It looks worse than it feels."

I cup her chin in my hand and make her look me in the eye. They look more normal now, but she's not out of the woods.

"Jenna, I'm *so sorry* this happened."

"I'm fine," she replies. "Or I will be in just a couple of days. Honest. It was an accident."

I feel helpless and like an ass on top of it, but I gather her in my arms again and walk into the steaming bathroom.

"Oh, this feels good," she says softly. I set her on her feet and wait until she gets her balance. "I'm okay."

"You're not going in there alone," I say. "I don't need you to fall."

"Probably a good idea, but there will be no post-accident sex today. Sorry, movie star."

"Very funny."

She stands fairly still as I lather up the cloth and gingerly run it over her skin, cleaning her.

"I don't need to wash my hair," she says. Her teeth are starting to chatter, so I rinse her off and leave the hot water running as I reach for a towel and lead her out onto the mat.

"Don't you want to turn that off?"

"No, it's keeping the room warmer," I reply as I quickly dry us both and then gather her back into my arms and return to the bedroom. "Where are your comfy clothes?"

"That dresser," she says, pointing. "Middle drawer."

"Got it." I find a cozy sweatshirt and matching sweatpants along with some panties and quickly get her dressed. "This will warm you up."

"I don't know why I'm cold."

"The adrenaline is wearing off," I reply. It's starting to wear off in me, too, but I don't have time to shake or fall apart.

I have to take care of *her*, and if I can just focus on that, I'll be fine.

"I don't have comfies for you," she says. "I'm sorry."

"I'll be fine. The blankets are heavy." I rush into the bathroom and turn off the water, then return to Jenna and peel the covers back to get her settled in the bed. She sighs happily. "Do you want tea?"

"I want sleep. And you."

I hurry under the covers, feeling cold myself, and she immediately wraps her arm around my waist and lays her head on my chest. I bury my nose in her hair and take a deep breath.

"Could have lost you today," I whisper, every word tearing through me.

"Don't talk like that," she says and kisses my

chest. "I'm okay."

But it's true. I *could* have lost her today, and I don't know what I would do if that were to ever happen.

I couldn't have lived with myself.

She's everything fresh and wonderful in my life.

***

"You're awake," I say, my voice quiet as I walk into the bedroom carrying a tray with hot tea and some crackers. "I don't have to wake you up."

"I missed you," she admits with a sleepy smile and sits up in the bed. She holds her forehead with her fingertips. "Ugh, the headache is the worst part."

"It's time for more meds," I reply as I set the tray on the bedside table and reach for the pills the emergency room sent home with us.

"I'd rather not."

"Rather not what, take the pills?"

She nods.

"Well, this is non-negotiable, fancy face. You need them to help you feel better. It's only for a couple of days."

"You're not the boss of me," she says, making me laugh.

"No, I doubt many are. But I'm putting my foot down on this one. We need you to heal, and resting comfortably is the only thing that will make that happen."

She frowns, but she doesn't say no when I offer her the medicine.

"Good girl."

"I don't usually like to be taken care of," she informs me.

"I know."

"But, thank you. It's comforting to have you here. My brothers would hover annoyingly. And my mom is great, but she's not nearly as nice to snuggle with as you are."

I crawl onto the bed and pass her a mug of coffee. This one says, *I asked for pizza, not your opinion.*

Her mugs crack me the fuck up.

"Are your parents in Arizona now?"

"Yeah." She takes a sip and then looks up at me in surprise. "This doesn't taste like shit."

"Well, halleluiah."

"Thanks." She takes another sip. "My parents are snowbirds. They head down right after Thanksgiving and then come back for Memorial Day."

"So I just missed them, then."

"You did. Brad will call and tell them what happened, and then I'll have to convince them not to come home just for this."

"They love you."

"Yeah. And they worry. Dad was a cop for a lot of years, so he's protective. And Mom is, well, a mom."

"I'm not close to my family," I reply, surprised to be talking about it. I never do. I've grown so used to not talking about myself over the years, I don't think about it.

But I enjoy sharing with Jenna.

"How come?"

"Oh, a million reasons. My dad's an alcoholic, and he's not a nice drunk. My mom left him when I was a kid when she moved us to L.A."

"So that's how that happened."

"Yeah. She was obsessed with making me a child actor."

"It worked."

"And she was the clichéd momager."

"Was she as bad as Lindsay Lohan's mom?"

"Oh, yeah. Just as bad. And she took a lot of my money, as well. Said she was just paying herself, but that's not what it was. She was stealing what I earned."

"Ugh, that fucking sucks." She takes my hand and kisses my fingers. "I'm sorry."

"It was a long time ago."

"Where is she now?"

"She still lives in L.A., last I heard. She has a nice house and all of the things she always wanted.

She just doesn't have me."

"Do you make sure she has those things?"

I frown. "You see too much."

"I'm learning you," she agrees. "You love her, and I could see you making sure she's okay, even if you don't want to see her. Is Nina close to her?"

"Not super close, but she sees her once in a while."

She nods and yawns, then nibbles on a cracker. "I'm getting sleepy again."

"Eat your cracker, and then you can sleep."

She does as I say, which is a testament to how out of it she is. I hate that the fight has gone out of her today.

I set our mugs aside, and we snuggle down into the covers again, falling asleep.

CHAPTER SIXTEEN

Jenna

"I'M BOOOOOOORED," I say and throw my head back on the couch about as dramatically as I possibly can.

"It's only been three days," Christian replies, his hands on his hips as he stares down at me in frustration. Not that he's said he's frustrated, but let's be honest, I'd be frustrated with me.

"Can't we just go up and get you some new clothes from the tree house? I need to look in on them. Max is *not* good at this stuff, and I have guests."

"I'm not driving you on that road again," he says, shaking his head. "No way, no how."

"It's settled, then." I stand and lean in to kiss his arm as I walk by. "I'll drive."

"Jenna," he says with a sigh, pushing his hand through his hair, which is definitely his signature

I'm-gonna-spank-you move.

"Christian, I *have* to go back up there. My business is up there. And you have to go up there because you have ski lessons and all of your things are there."

"I've cancelled the rest of the lessons," he replies, and my jaw drops. "I need to be available to you."

"I'm fine." I dance a fake jig and turn a circle, then hold my hands out and say, "Ta-da."

"Also, I *know* how to ski now. I feel confident that I'll do great in the film. I'm good on the skiing."

"Well, you still need your things."

"I can pay someone to gather them and bring them to me."

I roll my eyes and sigh heavily. "None of that changes the fact that my property is up there, and I have to work."

"Tomorrow." He walks to me and pulls me against him, rocking us back and forth. "Let's pretend like we don't have to go back up there for one more day."

"It's like getting back on a horse," I say, my words muffled by his chest. "You have to do it sometime. And aren't you sick to death of these clothes?"

"I just wash them every day."

"You're being silly."

His arms tighten around me. "It was the scariest thing I've ever been through, and I'd rather not repeat it."

"Well, we won't because we won't wreck again," I promise, rubbing soothing circles on his back. "It was a fluke, Christian. A complete accident."

"One more day," he repeats, kissing the top of my head and breathing me in. "You seem to be feeling better today."

"I'm much better. No headache. And my chest bruises are fading. I haven't even taken one pain pill today."

"I'm so glad." He kisses my head again, and I let my hand move down to his ass, copping a feel.

"If you're not going to take me somewhere, we could get naked."

He leans back to smile down at me. "Feeling *that* good?"

"Oh, yeah. I mean, have you felt this ass? It does things to me."

He smirks and lifts me easily into his arms, carrying me down the hall to my bedroom, the same way he did the other day after the accident.

Except this time, he's putting me to bed for completely different reasons.

He sets me on my feet, and I immediately tear into his shirt, trying to get it over his head.

"I need to get this thing off of you."

"You don't like it?"

"I'm sick of it," I reply with a grin. "I don't remember what you look like in anything else. It has to go."

I let it drop to the ground and smile in satisfaction.

"Better?" he asks.

"We're getting there. Now, these jeans."

"They're just jeans. They didn't hurt anybody."

I laugh as I push my finger under the waistband and let it travel back and forth, the back of my finger rubbing against his warm skin. His abs are tight, and goosebumps break out over his flesh.

"Do you like that?"

"I like everything you do."

I press my lips to his chest as I flip the button free from his jeans and work them over his hips. They pool around his feet, and he steps out of them, tossing them aside in the process.

My fingertip falls in the valley of that sexy V, and I bite my lip.

"Damn, you're hot. *People* magazine was right."

"Yours is the only opinion that matters," he says. He still hasn't touched me since he set my feet on the floor, so I take off my own clothes. His blue eyes immediately fall to the green and purple marks on my chest, and I see sadness in his gaze.

"Hey, my eyes are up here," I remind him, trying to lighten the mood.

"I'm so sorry, baby." He lifts his hand and gently brushes the pads of his fingers over the marks.

"Stop." My voice is firm, and his gaze flies to mine. "Stop feeling sorry. I'm not going to tell you again, it was an accident, and I feel *fine*. I'm not lying. There is nothing to forgive here. So please stop it and make love to me because a girl has *needs* when a sexy guy like you is standing in front of her."

"A sexy guy like me?" He swallows, and his face loosens into a smile. "I'm not sure I like that statement."

"No?"

He shakes his head, his lips twitching, and my funny, flirty man is back. He advances on me, and I back up so he can't touch me, moving toward the bed. The backs of my legs hit the mattress, and I sit, then crawl back. Christian follows me, crawling over me but not touching me.

It's fucking sexy.

"What should I have said?" My breath is coming faster. My heart has sped up.

Jesus, I want him.

"*You.*" He leans down and licks my nipple. That's the only point of contact, just his tongue on my nipple, and my whole body is on fire.

On. Fucking. Fire.

"I did say *you.*"

"You said *like you*, and that doesn't do it for me." He licks the other nipple, and I want his hands on me everywhere, but the stubborn man refuses to touch me. "It's just *me.*"

"Just you," I agree, my legs scissoring. "Now, touch me."

He kisses along my collarbone to my neck, to my sweet spot, and hangs out there, licking and nibbling.

"Christian, you're making me crazy."

"I don't want to hurt you," he admits.

"You won't hurt me. Ever." I cup his face in my hands. "I'm not fragile, damn it. I want your fingerprints on me, and I don't want you to be gentle."

His eyes narrow.

"Are you sure?"

Rather than answer, I kiss him and hitch my leg over his hip, practically climbing him. I'm not lying when I say that I feel great.

I need this with him. He's been gentle and sweet for three days, and now I need him to ravage my damn body.

He flips me over and pins my hips to the bed, my legs together, straddling me. He covers me, still kissing my neck as he pushes his hard cock between my ass cheeks.

"Now that's sexy," I breathe.

"No, you're the hot one. Your back is lean and firm. Your ass is perfect with two dimples in your low back." He spreads my cheeks open with his thumbs, and before I know it, he's easing himself inside me. "And since you asked for it, I'm going to leave a mark on you, right here."

His fingers dig into my ass, and he starts moving quickly, fucking me the way I asked. But I notice that he's not letting *me* do much work, which I know is his way of making sure we both get what we want.

I want it to be hard and fast and a bit wild.

And he wants to make sure he's taking care of me.

And I love him for it.

***

"I'm finally getting my ice cream," I say the next day as we stand in line at Sweet Scoops, waiting our turn. It seems we're not the only weirdos who like to eat ice cream in the winter.

"There are so many flavors to choose from," Christian says, staring at the menu. "What do you suggest?"

"Well, you can always go with the huckleberry. That's a staple in this town, and it's delicious. I love the grasshopper. And the cherry cherry quite contrary."

"So, what you're saying is, get a little of all of it."

I smile. "Exactly. Why don't we get a couple of pints to take up to the tree house? We can share them later while we watch movies."

"Sounds good."

We get three pints, all of the ones I recommended, and then drive up the hill. Christian's driving, and he's moving at a snail's pace.

"I know that you're taking it careful and all—"

"Do not complain about my speed," he says, his hands tightening on the wheel. This isn't a good time to remind him that ice doesn't care how fast you're going. "We'll get there eventually."

"Before I'm old and grey would be nice," I mumble, earning a glare from him. "I'm not in a hurry."

"When do the guests arrive?"

"In about an hour. I just want to take a look at the units to make sure that the cleaners did a good job and that Max didn't let anyone get away with murder."

"He's an intelligent man," he reminds me. "Some have said he's the most brilliant mind of our generation."

"Oh, God, don't say that around him. He'll walk around with a big head for weeks."

"I'm just saying that he's smart enough to figure it all out."

"I'm a control freak." I shrug and hold my breath as we pass by where our accident occurred.

A tow truck came to get his rental days ago, but you can still make out where it was in the snow-bank. We continue puttering up the hill, and I don't breathe a sigh of relief until we park at the tree houses and he cuts the engine. "Okay, you were right. That sucked."

"It'll get easier," he says and jumps out of my car, then walks around to help me out. "I'll go put the ice cream in my freezer while you check the units."

"Thanks. Don't eat it all without me."

"I don't want you to beat me up," he says and winks at me as I walk into the Ponderosa. It smells freshly cleaned. A quick walk-through reveals nothing worth noting, which is exactly what I was hoping.

I do the same walk-through in the Spruce unit, and I'm happy when it also comes up perfectly clean and ready for today's guests.

"How is it?" Christian asks from the doorway.

"They're great. Max and the cleaners did a good job."

"Told you." He taps the end of my nose and leads me to the Tamarack. "I'm going to change out of these offensive clothes."

"Thank the good Lord." He laughs as he walks away, and I immediately make myself a cup of de-caf. "You might want to burn those."

"No way, these are my favorite jeans."

I chuckle as I add sugar to my coffee and then jump when my phone pings with a text.

"Oh, that must be them."

Hey, Jenna. We're running a little late and would love it if there was dinner waiting for us in the unit. I'm happy to pay for it. Would pizza be something you could do?

"Is it them?"

I show Christian the text, and he frowns.

"Do many guests ask for that kind of service?"

I stare at him for a moment and then bust up laughing.

"If you remember correctly, you asked me about coffee and food when you got here."

"Yeah, I asked where I could get it, I didn't ask you to do it for me. That was just a bonus."

"Well, I do sometimes get these kinds of requests. I wouldn't mind getting the pizza, but I don't really want to have to drive down for it."

"No." He shakes his head adamantly. "Isn't there a place up here? We're still in the heart of ski season. Someone serves food."

"Excellent idea."

I make a phone call, and sure enough, the pub in the village serves pizza, and they're going to deliver three of them to the tree house within the hour.

"Okay, that's taken care of. I think I'll go wait for the pizza at the Ponderosa. Want to join me?"

He grins. "Of course. Give me five to make my own coffee."

It takes him three, and then we're walking the short distance to the other tree house. The snow has stopped falling, and it's not terribly cold out.

"Do you want to stand out on the deck for a bit?" I ask him.

"In the snow?"

I laugh and push up on my tiptoes to kiss him. "It's not snowing now. I just want to step out for a minute."

"Let's go."

We lean on the railing, sipping our coffee and watching skiers sail down the run to the village below.

"This is a fun spot," Christian says, just as a breeze kicks up.

"Damn, it's cold now. Let's go in." He shuts the door behind us, and I flip on the fireplace and sit on the couch. "How did you get this property?"

"That's actually a fun story," I reply and set my cup aside. "The property itself had been for sale for a long time, mostly because it was a weird shape. It butts up against the resort, and the way it was before, it was a weird triangle. Not great for building something like this.

"Well, thankfully, I know Jacob, and he owns said resort. So, I went to him and told him that I wanted to buy the property, but that we would need to rezone the property lines so I would give him a piece of my property in exchange for a piece of his, and he agreed."

"It's not what you know, it's who you know," he says with a smile.

"It's both." I hold up my mug in salute. "Jacob is a shrewd businessman. He knew that these tree houses would be beautiful and interesting to skiers. And he knew that I'd bring in more business for the resort, so it was a win-win situation."

"Sounds perfect," he says with a nod. "I see that there's another lot available for sale just below you."

"I've considered it, mostly because I'd like to make sure that no one can build on it and obstruct the view that I have here."

"That sounds completely reasonable. Why don't you buy it?"

I stare down into my mug. "Because I can't afford to yet. I had to invite Max and Brad to be investors in the tree houses. They went over budget, and it was more money than I had on hand. They both jumped on board. I just acquired the property in the park a few months ago, and I have a mortgage on that. So, until I have those paid off, I can't add more. It's too much."

"Jenna, I can—"

There's a knock on the door.

"That must be the pizza."

I jump up and set my mug on the kitchen island as I walk past it and pull the door open, then frown.

"Hi, I'm Nina. Is my brother here?"

CHAPTER SEVENTEEN

Jenna

I'M STRUCK DUMB. A petite brunette is standing in the doorway asking for Christian, and my brain doesn't want to connect the dots.

Why in the world is Nina *here*?

"Um, yeah," I reply and step back so she can come inside. "Christian," I call out as Nina walks inside, squeals, and gives her brother a hug.

"Hey," Christian says, looking at me over Nina's head with confused eyes. "What's going on?"

"Well, I was going to have to send the plane for you anyway, so I just came with it. I haven't seen you in too long." She steps back and looks around my tree house. "This is nice."

"Thanks," I reply.

"And you must be Jenna," she says, holding out her hand for mine. "Nice to meet you."

"Likewise." *I think.* "This is actually a unit that I'm filling later today with guests. Christian's is on the other side by the ski run."

She nods and hooks her dark hair behind her ear. "Well, this is definitely a great place. Christian, we need to get back to the plane right away."

"What the hell is going on?" he asks. "If you called or texted, I didn't get it."

"You didn't?" She scowls and checks her phone. "My text didn't go through."

"What the fuck is going on?" he asks again.

"Mom's in the hospital," she says. "I'm sorry you didn't get my text earlier. She had a heart attack during the night, and they think she's going to be okay, but we should probably get back."

I glance at Christian, whose jaw is clenched as he shoves his hand through his hair. He looks frustrated, but not particularly sad or worried about his mom. Maybe he's just taken off guard?

"You left your mom after she had a heart attack?" I ask, unable to keep the words inside, and Nina turns to me with glacial blue eyes.

"You don't know me," she says, her voice heavy in warning. "You don't get to question my choices."

"Sorry." I hold up my hands in surrender, and then the reality of the moment hits me.

He's leaving.

Today.

Not in a week.

Christian crosses to me and grips my shoulders before tipping his forehead to mine. "I'm so sorry, Jenna."

"Hey, it's your mom. Of course, you have to go."

His face is covered in torment, so I wrap my arms around him and hug him tightly, trying to re-assure him.

"She's going to be okay."

He presses his lips to my ear. "Are *you* going to be okay?"

"Of course." I pull back and give him my best, bright smile because if I do anything else, I'll break down into tears, and no one wants that. "I'm al-ways okay, remember?"

"You'd better go pack," Nina says.

Christian kisses me softly, then pulls away and hurries out the door, shutting it behind him.

"Did you really try to text him?" I ask, not turn-ing around to look at Nina. I can't put my finger on it, but there's something about all of this that I just don't trust.

"Of course, not," she says. "I hopped on the plane and came straight here to get him."

"Why?"

I turn now and find her sitting on the couch, her legs crossed and arm resting along the back of the sofa.

"Because I wanted the opportunity to have a little girl-to-girl chat with you."

I sit across from her. "Well, here we are."

She smiles. Nina is a beautiful woman with dark features, light blue eyes, and a slender figure. Her smile is sweet, showing off a dimple in her right cheek.

But her eyes are shrewd.

"It seems that you and my brother have started a little romance," she begins and looks down at her nails. "And don't get me wrong, I'm as much of a romantic as the next girl. I think it's sweet. But it can't last."

I don't even move a muscle in my face. I won't let her see anything that I'm thinking. I refuse to give her that.

"You don't know him," she continues, "you only know what you've seen over the past few weeks. But you don't know what it's really like to be attached to Christian. He's bigger than life itself. His life is demanding, grueling. And he doesn't have time to give to any kind of long-term relationship. Why do you think he's never done it before? Because, trust me, there have been opportunities."

"Maybe his sister sabotaged it." I tilt my head to the side, considering her. "And is sabotaging it now."

She narrows her eyes. "I love my brother very much, and I know what's best for him, and it's not some little snow bunny in BFE. What, did you think you'd get married and have a whole flock of babies?"

She laughs humorlessly and tucks her hair back again.

"Not gonna happen, sweetie. So, here's what I suggest. You just file this all away in your memories from that time you got to roll around in bed with the hot guy you used to cut out of *Teen Beat* as a kid, and you move on with your life. Trust me, as soon as we get on that plane headed back to L.A., Christian will forget all about this and you. He did what he came here to do: learn to ski and fuck a willing girl."

I blink rapidly, letting that settle in. Jesus, Nina is a first-class, grade-A bitch. I'm protective of my brothers, but even I wouldn't take it this far.

However, she's also not completely wrong. My life is completely different from Christian's, and I never truly believed that we could mesh our worlds together.

I hoped, but we never talked about it, not really. There was wishful thinking because we were in our bubble together.

We just enjoyed the days we had together, and I expected to have a few more of them.

It's just getting cut short, that's all.

And, oh my, how it hurts.

"What it boils down to," Nina continues, "is that Christian is a full-time job for everyone around him. You're a businesswoman, Jenna. If you come to L.A. with him, you'll have to give up a lot of your life here. Because you know he's not going to give up his career for you. He simply can't."

Christian walks into the unit, and Nina immediately stands, smiling at him.

"I'll meet you down at the car. We have to leave as soon as possible. Bye, Jenna."

She leaves, shutting the door behind her, and Christian crosses to me, squats before me, and cups my face.

"I hate that I'm leaving, but we can make this work. You can come down to L.A. right after Christmas. I have to do a premiere appearance, and I'd love to take you as my date. I'll have dresses brought in and—"

"No," I interrupt him and kiss his palm, then pull it from my face. "Christian, I won't be coming to L.A. We never talked about the future, and I always knew that we just had these few weeks together."

He frowns. "What the hell are you talking about? I love you, Jenna. Of course, I want you to join me in L.A."

"And then what?" I ask, anger and frustration setting up residence in my chest. I don't know if I'm angry at Nina or Christian right now. Or if I simply feel like a fool because I let myself believe in the fairy tale. "I follow you around like a love-sick puppy? I have a business here in Montana, Christian. My family is here. My *life* is here. I can't just leave all that and go to L.A."

"I'm not telling you to leave it permanently. I'm not a dick, Jenna. I just need you to meet me halfway here."

Nina lays on the horn down below, and Christian swears under his breath.

"I know," I reply with a nod. "You wouldn't ask me to do that, but that's what would eventually happen because your job is important, and your life is this big...*thing*. And that's not what I want."

"So what are you saying, Jenna?"

"That it was so wonderful to spend this time with you," I whisper and lean forward to kiss his lips softly. "And you will forever be written on my heart, but this can't really go anywhere."

"Jenna, this is ridiculous."

"No. It's not ridiculous. Both of our lives are important, we've said that from the beginning. I don't want to give up my life."

"For the record," he says as he leans in, his blue eyes sad and frustrated, "I'm not asking you to give up your life. Not once did I ask you to do that. But if you'd like to walk away, well, I don't know how to convince you otherwise right now, and I have to go. But, Jenna, this isn't over."

He shakes his head and heads to the doorway, then looks back at me before walking out the door and closing it softly behind him—walking right out of my life.

I'm numb, not able to move for long minutes as I hear the car start and pull away from the tree houses. This hurts worse than anything I've ever been through. I don't think I've ever known this kind of deep, searing pain. Even the concussion from the accident didn't hurt like this.

It feels like someone has reached inside my chest and torn out my heart.

I love Christian, and I can't have him. He was never really mine. He was on loan from his real life, and now he's gone, and I won't ever see him again.

Jesus, I won't ever see him again.

I bury my face in my hands and let the tears come, every one of them hot with grief and pain.

It seems like hours later when there's a knock on the door.

I walk on numb legs and open it to find a young kid holding hot pizza.

"Hi, Miss Jenna. Here are your pizzas. Hey, are you okay?"

I nod, brushing tears from my cheeks. "Of course. I was chopping onions. Thanks, kiddo. Did you put this on my tab?"

"Yes, ma'am."

I tip him and turn back into the kitchen.

And now it's time to get to work.

***

It's been ten days since I last saw his face. Touched him. Made love with him.

Ten long, agonizing days.

I thought it would get better with time, but that hasn't been the case. I've buried myself in work, had Christmas with my brothers a couple of days ago, and now, my friends have insisted that I come back to the land of the living.

I'm meeting Grace, Hannah, and Willa at Dress It Up for coffee and girl-talk before Willa opens for the day.

I'm in charge of picking up the caffeine, so I swing into Drips & Sips and get in line.

"Jenna."

I turn at the deep voice and am immediately swept up into a big hug. Noah King has been a friend of mine since grade school. He's sweet, soft-spoken, and owns the birds of prey sanctuary just outside of town.

"Hey, Noah." I lean back to smile up at him but don't pull out of his arms. The hug feels nice. "How are you?"

"I'm great." His brown eyes narrow as he *really* looks at me. "And you're sad."

"I'm not sad at all."

"Liar." He lets me go and tucks his hands into his pockets. "Did you have a good Christmas?"

"Oh, yeah, Brad and Max spoiled me a bit with some new fancy shoes." I wink at him. "I'll keep them. How about you?"

"I did. You know how big and crazy the King holidays are."

"You do have a huge family," I agree as I'm called up to place my order. "It was good to see you, Noah."

"You too, Jenna. Take care."

I place our order and hurry down the block in the cold to Willa's shop. I knock on the glass door, and Willa rushes over to let me in.

"Man, it's cold outside," I say, shaking snowflakes out of my hair. Willa takes the coffees from me and sets them on the counter by the cash register. Grace and Hannah both come bouncing out from the back of the store.

"I'm buying these," Grace announces, holding up a pair of shoes. "I'm fairly certain that I'll be able to wear them after the pregnancy."

"I didn't know we were here to shop," I say and take a sip of my coffee, then sigh with happiness.

"We *always* shop," Grace says with a laugh. "But now we're here to chat."

"This is kind of an intervention," Willa says.

"I know." I sigh and take my coat off and hang it on the end of a nearby rack. "You guys aren't exactly stealthy about these things."

"We love you," Grace says. "And we're worried about you."

"You haven't said *anything* about Christian

leaving. You've just worked yourself into exhaustion," Hannah adds. "And that's not healthy."

"Why did he leave early?" Willa asks. "Did you fight?"

"No." I sip my coffee. "His mom had a heart attack, and his sister came to fetch him."

"So you're still talking to him? Is his mom okay?"

"No, I'm not still talking to him." I pace around the shop, unable to stand still. "He wanted me to come to L.A. after Christmas, but I told him no. My life is here, guys. What am I going to do, just follow him around? I can't do that, I wouldn't be able to respect myself. So, I told him the truth, that we always knew this had an expiration date, and it arrived earlier than we'd planned."

"Wow," Grace says. "And he said *fuck that* and swept you up into his arms and confessed his undying love and said that he'd make it all work out, right?"

I shake my head no.

"His sister was right. I don't really know him, I only know what he showed me while he was here. I got to play make believe with the guy I thought was hot when I was a kid and now I have to move on."

"Wait." Hannah holds her hand up, stopping me. "Did she actually *say* that?"

"Pretty much."

"Was Christian there when she said it?"

"No." I toss my empty coffee cup into the garbage and immediately wish for more. "He was packing his things so he could go back to his fancy life in L.A. You guys, this is all for the best. I love my life here. This is my home."

"But you're *in* love," Grace says softly, her eyes full of tears.

"Sometimes, being in love isn't enough." I shrug. "And I love you all for being worried about me, but I'm going to be okay. I'm sad, that's for sure. And I'm a little irritated with myself for falling for him in the first place."

"Don't do that," Willa says, reaching out to take my hand. "Don't beat yourself up for falling in love. It doesn't happen often, and it seemed like he was really good to you."

"He was." Tears threaten again. "But I just don't see how something can work between us. We're from two different universes, you guys. He's a superstar who lives in a fifteen-thousand-square-foot house in Beverly Hills. He jets all over the world, in a private plane, I might add—"

"Your brother has a private plane," Hannah interjects. "I've been on it. It's awesome."

"It's not *mine*. And I don't identify with a lot of Max's life either. I'm not into designer things. I love pretty shoes, but I couldn't tell the difference between Chanel and Gucci to save my life."

"I can help with that," Willa says with a grin.

"I'd be happy to."

"You know what I'm trying to say." I sigh, the fight having gone out of me. "I am not celebrity wife material, and Christian deserves that."

"Seems to me, Christian deserves to be happy with whoever sets his soul on fire," Grace says with a shrug. "There are celebrities who are married to civilians. Matt Damon and his wife have like a dozen kids."

"You can hire help with your properties," Hannah says. "And it's not like Christian is filming or promoting all the damn time. There's plenty of time that he's off and can be here with you. You can follow *each other* around."

"I love you guys. I do. So much. But you aren't going to fix this." But they do have good points that I've considered myself the past couple of days.

But isn't it too late?

"Well, we tried," Hannah replies and pulls me in for a big hug. "And we're always here for you, no matter what."

"Thank you."

Once in my car, I check my phone and frown when I see that I missed a text from Christian. It's simple.

Please talk to me. I miss you.

God, I miss him, too. So much. And I'm not convinced that I did the right thing. I reacted to Nina, and I admit that I was scared of the idea of what life would look like once Christian left. I had gotten so good at living in the moment that I panicked when it came to thinking ahead.

I think it might have been the worst mistake of my life.

***

I'm wrapped in blankets on my couch, watching TV and scrolling through social media on my phone.

Cara King posted photos of all of the kiddos on the ranch, and I give it a heart. Man, Zack's son Seth is growing so fast. He's as tall as his dad and uncle now, and it looks like he'll keep growing.

Lauren's author page is promoting her newest book, which I already have signed and on my shelf. Maybe I'll read it this weekend. We're supposed to get a hell of a blizzard, so cuddling up by the fire with one of Lauren's books sounds like a good idea.

I keep scrolling and then laugh out loud at the picture of Noah King holding an eagle that's flapping its wings in his face. It was good to see Noah the other day. I tap the laughing icon on his photo, and then the voice on the TV catches my attention.

"—Christian Wolfe and Serena Holmes arrived at the premiere of *Tender Graces* tonight, looking as in love as ever."

"That's right, Meghan, it seems that the media coverage of a short fling with an unknown woman was all just hype because Christian escorted Serena to the premiere, and as you can see, they're looking pretty cozy."

"Serena is wearing de la Renta."

"Man, is she! That blue is just stunning with her eyes. And let's not overlook how absolutely sexy Christian is in his Armani tuxedo."

I can't take my eyes off Christian. He's smiling for the cameras, his arm around Serena's waist, and his other hand tucked into his pocket.

He looks *so* handsome.

My phone rings in my hand.

"Hello?"

"It's Natalie. Are you watching the red carpet?"

"Yeah."

"Well, stop it. You know it's not real. They're not really a couple at all. I'm calling to fight those voices in your head that are making you question things right now."

"It's okay, Nat. It doesn't matter if it's real or not. We aren't together anymore."

"What? Oh, honey. What happened?"

I'm so sick of this question.

"It just wasn't going to work," I reply and turn off the TV. "We're too different. And I know you're going to call bullshit because you and Luke have made it work so well, but we aren't you, Nat."

"I know you're not us," she says softly. "I was just really pulling for you guys. I think you were good for each other. Hold on."

She takes the phone away from her mouth, but I can hear every word she's saying.

"She and Christian broke up. She just said it wasn't going to work. I don't know." She comes back on the line. "Luke says he's sorry, too."

"You guys are so nice," I say and brush a tear off my cheek.

"Are you absolutely sure it's over? Because, frankly, I think you're being hasty."

"Oh, yeah." I laugh humorlessly and reach for a tissue. "I was reminded that I don't fit in that world."

"By who?"

"His sister."

"God save me from overprotective sisters," she mutters. "Maybe that's exactly what it was, Jenna. If it came from Nina and not Christian, he may not feel the same way."

"She wasn't wrong," I reply with a shrug. "I'm on the mend. I have plenty to keep me busy."

"Well, add house hunting to that list because Luke and I are going to buy a place out there so our family can come and vacation. We just fell in love with it."

I smile, excited at the thought of having Natalie nearby some of the year. "That would be awesome, and I'm happy to help. I'm not an agent, but I have an excellent one. I'll hook you up, and I'll check out anything you're interested in."

"You're the best." Luke says something in the background again. "I have to go. Call if you need anything."

"Thanks, Nat." We hang up, and I lean my head back. I'm tired of crying. I'm tired of missing Christian.

I'm just tired.

When will it get better?

CHAPTER EIGHTEEN

Christian

Ten Days Ago…

"**A**RE YOU OKAY?" Nina asks. She's sitting opposite me in the private jet, and we're flying away from Cunningham Falls to L.A.

Away from Jenna.

Everything in me wants to tell the pilot to turn around and get me back there. To pull Jenna into my arms and make her see that we can make this work and she's the only person I want in my life.

But I can't forget the cold way she dismissed me. As if she'd shut the emotions off altogether.

If they were real in the first place.

They had to be real, there's no way I imagined all that.

"Fine."

"You don't seem fine. Was your goodbye sad? Aren't you going to see her again?"

"I don't know." I slug down half a bottle of water.

"I'm sorry, Christian. But it's probably for the best. I mean, your worlds are so different, and California is pretty far from Montana."

I just nod, wishing my sister would shut the fuck up. I'm quite sure that we could have worked around the geography. And I would have taken the next couple of days to talk to Jenna, to make plans for the future. I was just too selfish with our private little bubble to talk about what would happen after the bubble popped.

And now I'm gone, and she doesn't want to see me again.

I look out the window to the dark clouds below and bite my lip, ignoring my sister who's still talking. She's pulled out her planner and is rattling off my schedule, full of meetings and photo shoots and television appearances.

The full onslaught of promotion is about to start. Ready or not.

"First, we'll go see Mom, of course," she says.

"I haven't seen her in five years."

"I know." She sets her planner on her lap and frowns. "I know there are hard feelings there, Chris, but damn it, she could have *died*. Shouldn't you let bygones be bygones and try to have a relationship with Mom?"

"Fifteen million dollars," I murmur, and she grimaces.

"I know."

"It wasn't your money, and you weren't the one she betrayed. I understand and support you wanting to be close with her, Nina. I do. But I don't have the desire to have the same kind of relationship. So, I'll stop by and say hello, and then I'm going home to get ready for this press junket."

"Understood," she replies, and I turn away, pulling out my phone and connecting to the on-board Wi-Fi.

I bring up my browser, find the land for sale in front of Jenna's mountain property, and contact the agent.

Dear Sir,

I would like to purchase this property. I've already seen it, so no need to take me out there. Please advise on how you'd like to proceed. I'll pay full asking price.

Sincerely,

Christian Wolfe

***

I do *not* want to do this.

I've made it through the past ten days without feeling much of anything. I'm a robot. I saw my mother, and that went as well as it always does.

Full of frustration and mistrust.

Thankfully, she's recovering at home, and Nina is looking in on her.

I've been in New York and London to promote *Tender Graces,* and now we're back in L.A. for the premiere tonight.

The movie is already garnering huge critical acclaim, and my name has been thrown around with the possibility of another Oscar nod.

And I don't care.

I'm sitting in the back of a stretch limo with Serena Holmes perched as far away from me as humanly possible. We haven't said two words to each other on this tour when it wasn't in front of a camera.

We can't stand each other.

But we're really, really good at faking it.

"I can't wait until this is all done so I don't have to do this with you anymore," she hisses between her teeth, glaring at me.

"Sweetheart, I couldn't agree more." I watch the crowds on either side of the car. No one can see inside, which is good.

I don't want to have to touch her more than necessary.

When we park in front of the red carpet, Serena slides over to me, plasters on her fake smile, and we climb out of the car. I turn to offer her my hand and escort her down the carpet, stopping on our marks to smile for the cameras.

A thousand lights are flashing around us, video cameras are pointed at us, and every gossip columnist has a mic in their hands, hasty to thrust them in our faces as we approach.

Serena lets me do most of the talking, per the studio's request. She wasn't happy with that, but they're paying her paycheck, so it is what it is.

I assume my normal stance, one arm slung around her low back, and my other hand tucked into my pocket. The crowd is deafening, and the lights are blinding.

This used to excite me. It pumped up my adrenaline, and I *lived* for moments like these, when all eyes were on me, and the people couldn't wait to hear what I had to say.

And now, well, I don't enjoy it like I once did. I even resent it.

I need a break from it.

"Let's go," Serena says in my ear, making it look like she's kissing my cheek. "These lights are giving me a fucking headache."

I don't say a word as I gesture for her to go ahead of me, and I follow behind, careful not to step on the train of her dress.

That happened in New York, and I got the verbal beating of a lifetime when we got back into the limo on the way to the hotel once the after party was finished.

She's fucking exhausting.

Serena and I won't be watching the film to-night. Instead, we'll come back for the after party, and then I'm *done*. There isn't a European leg of this tour, thank God.

I don't have anything until I report to Vancouver to start filming Luke's movie in February.

What I'm going to do with a month on my hands, I have no idea.

Except, I want to go to Jenna. To talk some sense into her and find out what really happened that last day because I don't believe for a second that she just turned off her feelings like a light switch.

***

"You should go somewhere tropical," Nina says the following morning. We're having breakfast in my outdoor space, which overlooks downtown and all the way to the ocean.

The view is killer.

"Not in the mood."

She sighs and takes a bite of her fruit, looking at stuff on her computer. I'm reading the newspaper, trying to ignore her. I'd rather be alone, but she won't leave.

"You can't keep moping," she says. "Christian, you're starting to worry me."

"Don't worry about me," I reply, shaking my head. "I'm fine. I just don't want to go somewhere fucking tropical. Why, do *you* want to go and you're hoping you can tag along?"

"I mean, that wouldn't suck." She bats her eyelashes, but I don't think it's funny. "Are you just going to mope around here until it's time to go to Vancouver? Jesus, you just spent weeks in the frigid cold, I would think you'd be clamoring for somewhere warm."

"We're sitting outside, aren't we? It's warm enough in L.A."

"You're so damn moody." She returns to the computer, and a few moments later, I hear, "uh-oh."

"What?"

"Well, you're going to see it sooner or later, so I guess I'll be the one to show you."

She flips the computer around to face me, and there on the screen are side-by-side photos. One of me kissing Jenna's cheek in Sweet Scoops, and the other of her hugging and smiling up at a strange guy in Drips & Sips.

The headline says, Brokenhearted ex-lover of Christian Wolfe has moved on!

"What the fuck," I mutter and skim the article. It's one paragraph about how she was spotted getting cozy with some guy in Cunningham Falls.

"She moved on pretty quickly," Nina says, and I glare at her, shutting her up.

My blood is on fire. Every muscle in my body

tense and ready to deck someone.

I stand and pace the patio, then stop and stare at the view.

None of this is worth a damn without Jenna.

"I mean, it hasn't even been two weeks."

"Shut the fuck up, Nina." I whirl around, and her eyes are wide. "Jesus, just shut up. I *love* her, and you're just talking about her like she's meaningless. She's not."

"Christian—"

"No. Stop talking. I've had it up to my fucking neck with you talking shit about her. I don't know what your deal is, but you got your wish. We're not together. But I don't need you rubbing it in my face every damn day."

"That's not what I'm doing."

"Yes. It is. And I've had it."

"Have you tried calling her?"

"I've called. I've texted. She won't answer me." I pace away again, frustrated. "It's like something happened, and a switch was thrown. She went from loving and affectionate to completely closed-off from me, and I don't know what happened because she *won't talk to me.*"

"Well," Nina says, and I turn at the sound of her voice. It's weaker, the way it is when she's about to confess something. "I might know what happened."

"What, Nina?"

"I said something to her."

"When?"

"When you went to pack your things." She swallows hard. "Christian, she's not meant for your life. She's a small-town girl, and you're *People* magazine's sexiest man alive. How could that ever work out?"

"Who the fuck are you to decide that we're not right for each other?"

She cringes, but I don't stop.

"Jesus, Nina, you're my manager and my sister, but you're not my keeper. You don't make my life decisions for me, and you just sabotaged the best thing that has ever happened to me. You don't even *know* her."

"I know that she made you forget your responsibilities," she fights back, standing from the chair at the table. "You never would have let someone take a video of you kissing someone before. You *know* what shit like that can do to your image, and you were finally recovering from the DUI shit storm."

"That shit storm was my *life*. But you don't care. All you care about is my image and what it does to my bottom line."

"That's not true."

"It's exactly true. I love you, Nina, but maybe I've given you too much say in what happens in my life."

"Christian, I didn't know that she meant that much to you. It's not like you called to talk to me about it. I saw everything through the press, and it looked like she was worming her way into your life and causing you to make mistakes. We can't have mistakes. And don't forget, I've spent my *entire life* watching people around you try to take a piece of you, including our own mother. I *am* your manager and sister, and goddamn it, I'm your protector."

"I'm a fucking human being!" I throw my hands into the air and stare at her like she's crazy. "Of course, I make mistakes, Nina. And let me just tell you right now, Jenna is *not* a mistake. She is amazing. She works hard, and she doesn't want to ride on my or anyone's coattails. I don't need to be protected from her. Her brother is Max Hull."

Nina's eyes widen again. "Really?"

"Yes. She already has access to more money than she'd ever need, but she doesn't ever ask her brother for a handout. She works her ass off, and her business isn't just successful, it kicks ass. You saw the tree houses."

"They *are* really cool."

"Fuck, Nina, what did you do?"

"I'm sorry." Her voice wobbles, but it's not enough to soften me up. "I overstepped."

"Understatement of the fucking year."

I pace away from her, pushing my hands through my hair. Jenna didn't send me away because she doesn't love me.

My idiot sister talked her into believing that she's not good enough for me.

And that pisses me off. I'm angry with both of them.

"Just to play Devil's advocate here," Nina says. "What does it say about her that she let a couple of words from me end things between you?"

"Nina, I know you. You can be ruthless, so I'm going to guess that it wasn't a few innocent words."

She swallows hard.

"Did you tell her that she's not good enough?"

"Maybe."

She sighs. "Okay, I fucked up. Bad."

I shake my head and reach for my phone.

"We need to fix this," she continues, already typing on her computer. "I'll call the plane, and you can fly out today."

"I don't want you to touch this," I reply coldly. "You're not fired, yet. But I'm not ready to forgive you."

"Christian."

"No. You've got to learn that you don't control me or any aspect of my life except my schedule. That's it. I'm going to get to Jenna. Today. And I'll deal with you later."

"I'm so sorry," she says, gathering her things. "Please don't stay mad at me."

"You told the love of my life to get lost. I'm

going to be mad for a while."

***

I can't get to her.

Cunningham Falls is under the blizzard of the century. No planes are leaving or landing right now, and it's not supposed to let up for another three days.

Three fucking days.

Every day since I left her has been misery, and now it's only worse because the cell towers are down, and I can't call her.

Besides, what I have to say needs to be said in person. Not over the phone where she can just hang up on me.

No, I need to look into her eyes and touch her skin. I need to *see* her.

So, I make arrangements for the plane to leave first thing as soon as the storm clears, get dressed, and start to head to Rodeo Drive to do some shopping but then stop short.

I can't be recognized when I do this, and I don't know where else to go.

Fuck.

I call Nina.

"If you're still mad at me, I'm hanging up."

"I'm *so* mad at you, but I need to set that aside for right now. I need your help."

"What's up?"

"I need to buy an engagement ring without the paparazzi finding out."

She's quiet.

"Nina?"

"Wow." She sniffles. "Christian, this is *so great.*"

"I haven't asked her yet. She's still not speaking to me, but I can't get to her for a couple of days, so that gives me time to get ready. Now, where do I go to get a fucking ring?"

"I know just the place. Pick me up."

I'm at her place in fifteen minutes, and she jumps into my little convertible with a smile on her pretty face.

"Which direction?" I ask.

"We're headed to Long Beach. There's a Cartier there. The one on Rodeo Drive will be swarming with the paps."

"You could have just told me this on the phone."

"Yes, but then I wouldn't get to help you pick it out, and that would just be sad."

The drive to Long Beach takes forever, thanks to traffic, and parking isn't exactly a breeze. But we're finally in the store, and I'm suddenly completely overwhelmed.

I have no idea what Jenna would like.

"Good afternoon," the saleswoman says. "I'm Genevieve, and I'm happy to help you today."

"I'm looking for an engagement ring. I hope I can trust that this is a confidential visit."

Genevieve raises a brow. "Of course. Is this your special lady?"

Nina chuckles. "No, I'm the meddling sister. I'm just here to help."

"Excellent. I'm sure we have something perfect for her. May I see a photo?"

I nod and thumb through the photos on my phone, find the one of Jenna and me at the ice skating rink, and show it to her.

"Oh, she's just lovely."

"Yes. She is."

"What does she do for a living?"

"She's in real estate, and she's sometimes in the middle of construction zones."

"So, she would need something that doesn't snag," Genevieve says as she pulls an open red velvet box from under the counter and then goes in search of a couple of rings to show me. "And correct me if I'm wrong, but she looks like a classy woman. Someone who would enjoy something traditional and simple."

"I think so," I reply with a nod.

Genevieve returns with five rings in different styles, but I know it as soon as I see it.

"This." I point to a ring with a massive diamond, set down in a halo of more diamonds.

"I thought you might like this," she says, pulling it out and passing it to me. "This one doesn't have any prongs, so it won't snag on anything. And it's simply beautiful."

"Oh, I love it," Nina breathes.

"The diamond is a cushion cut, and every diamond surrounding is a round cut and chosen by hand. The total karat weight is five karats."

Nina whistles, and I toss her a grin.

"We'll take it."

"Don't you want to know the price?" Genevieve asks.

"I don't care," I reply honestly. "This is her ring. I'll take it."

"Excellent." Genevieve takes it back and sets it in a red ring box. "I'll be happy to wrap it up for you."

"They do a great job with packaging," Nina says with a nod, but I shake my head no.

"It'll go in my pocket," I reply. "She won't open it like a gift."

"Of course." Genevieve nods. "I'll just have to fill out your certificate of authenticity, and with this large of a transaction, we wire the money directly from your bank."

"I understand."

Two hours and three coffees later, Jenna's ring is tucked safely in its box in my pocket, and I'm driving back to Beverly Hills.

Now, to get to my girl so I can make her mine permanently.

CHAPTER NINETEEN

Jenna

"**T**HIS LEMON POPPY SEED is to *die for*," Grace says as she pulls her fork out of her mouth and eyes the next piece of wedding cake on her plate. "But this strawberry looks amazing, too."

"The strawberry goes so well with the white chocolate ganache," Maisey Henderson, the owner and baker of the wedding cakes says with a wink. Her sister, Brooke, is pulling samples of flowers to show Hannah, as well.

We're in Brooke's Blooms, the hottest new flower shop in town. Brooke also sells pretty gifts and cards, and I've decided that I need to come in here more often. They've done an amazing job of making today special for Hannah, with a pretty bouquet on our table that Hannah gets to take with her, and a congratulatory cake for her to take home, as well. They've absolutely gone the extra mile, and I'll happily recommend them to other friends in the future.

"I can't believe that we're at the tail end of the blizzard of the century outside, and yet it feels like springtime in here," Hannah says, taking a deep breath. "It's just *so pretty.*"

"This is such a breath of fresh air," Willa says. "I'm so sick of being in my house."

"You should host parties here," I suggest and take a bite of the chocolate mousse and immediately sigh in happiness. "I'd come in for flowers and cake every week."

"That's actually a great idea, and something we're working on," Maisey says with a wink. "Hannah, you need to try this huckleberry filling."

"I want huckleberry filling, too," Grace says, making us all laugh.

"Trust the pregnant woman to like *everything*," Hannah says, rubbing Grace's round belly. "I'm only serving about a hundred people, Grace, not a thousand. I won't need that much cake."

"I'll take home the leftovers," Grace says with a laugh.

I love my friends, and I'm so happy for Hannah and that she found the love of her life. She and Brad fit so well together, and being a part of their special day is an honor.

I will *not* let my own sadness interfere with having fun with my friends today.

"Willa, what do you think of the peonies?" Hannah asks, pointing to the book. "I wish they were in season so we could see them in person."

"Peonies are always a yes," Willa replies, nodding emphatically while munching on her cake. "And, of course, some lilies."

"Let me show you a bouquet that I did a couple of years ago," Brooke suggests, typing on her laptop. "I have a folder on Pinterest with previous designs, and you're welcome to go look anytime. Here we go."

She turns the computer around, and we all sigh, immediately falling in love with the different shades of pink in the romantic bouquet.

"Oh, that's perfect," Hannah says. "Can you do this?"

"Absolutely," Brooke says. "I'll have to order in a few of the flowers from South America because they won't quite be in season here yet, but we can make it work."

Brooke is a few years younger than me, and I don't know her well, but she's *so* nice. And beautiful, with the darkest hair I've ever seen, and big brown eyes. She's petite and has a mole above her lip, Cindy Crawford style.

Maisey could be her twin, minus the mole, but I believe they're about a year apart in age.

"Okay, we need the lemon poppy seed with the huckleberry filling," Hannah says. "And I think the raspberry swirl with the white chocolate ganache."

"You're speaking my language," I say, taking another bite. "Being a bridesmaid is awesome. I get free cake, and I get to help pick out all the girlie things."

"I can't believe we're six weeks out from the wedding," Willa says.

"Thanks for waiting until I had the baby," Grace says.

"So many life changes this past year," I add and smile happily at my girls. "I'm so happy for you guys."

"Do *not* make me cry," Grace says. "I cry at everything these days. My hormones are out of control. I need this baby to come out."

"Soon," Hannah says. "Okay, it looks like we have the cake and the flowers figured out. Brooke, you guys are awesome."

"Oh, we know," Maisey says with a wink. "But, thank you. We're just thrilled for you, Hannah."

"And I made up a little something for each of you," Brooke adds, walking into the cooler. She comes back holding three smaller versions of the bouquet she made for Hannah. "We couldn't let you walk away without something pretty."

"Oh, thank you." I bury my nose in a rose and breathe deeply. "This *does* smell like spring, and I think that's something we all need right now."

"It's been a long winter," Hannah agrees. "Thank you, ladies."

"You're welcome," Brooke says. "And don't worry about any of this. We have it handled, and I've already coordinated with your venue to get all of the details worked out. Don't give us another thought."

"You're seriously the best," Willa says and picks up a tiny piece of cake to go. "I'll eat this on my walk back to the shop."

We wave goodbye to Brooke and Maisey and leave the flower shop, pausing on the sidewalk to exchange hugs.

"I'm going to help Grace to her car," I announce, taking Grace's hand in mine. The snow is still falling in big, heavy flakes. "I don't trust this clumsy pregnant girl on the ice."

"Good plan," Hannah says. "Thanks so much for coming, you guys. This whole wedding planning process has been fun because of you, and I love you."

"It's going to be a beautiful wedding," Grace replies before we all go our separate ways. I walk Grace to her car and make sure she's carefully inside before I walk to my own and head home.

All three tree houses are full on the mountain this week, so I have nothing to do up there. In fact, all of my properties are currently rented out, which makes me a happy business owner.

And on a snowy day like this, I have two options. I can go home and be sad on the couch, or I can go to my park property and be sad there.

It's no contest. Now that the roads are open, I'm excited to get back up there. I haven't been since I showed it to Christian.

It's the best place to think.

***

Well, that didn't work out the way I thought it would. The road into the park was still closed from the storm, so I had to turn around and go back home.

But at least I wasn't wallowing in my own self-pity on the couch, and that's a step in the right direction.

I have been, however, making myself crazy with self-doubt and frustration. I didn't know that I could miss someone so much. My whole body aches with it. I shouldn't have listened to Nina, and I should have talked to Christian. I should have *trusted* him.

I should have been brave.

I turn onto my street and frown at the SUV parked in front of my house. I don't recognize it.

I pull into my driveway, step out of my car, and when I turn around, my heart lodges in my throat.

Unless the snow is playing tricks on me, or my brain injury from the accident has resurfaced, Christian is walking across the snow toward me. My feet are planted, and I'm unable to move as he approaches and stops an arm's length away.

"Hi." His voice is rough, full of emotion, and

his blue eyes are hungrily taking me in.

"Hello." I shake myself out of my trance and reach back into the car for my handbag and the bouquet of flowers. He shuts the door for me and follows me to the house.

"You're not parking in the garage?"

"The door opener broke, and I haven't had a chance to call someone."

Are we really talking about my garage door? I want to jump on him, wrap my arms around him, and hold on so tightly that he can't ever go away again.

But that's not possible.

I lead him inside and set my flowers down while I shed my jacket and boots, then I turn to him. He's hovering inside the door, the same way he did that very first day when he arrived at the tree house early.

But this time, I don't know why he's here.

"Thanks to the fucking blizzard, it took me three days to get here, and I have some things to say." He clears his throat and looks down at the floor, and I've never been so happy to see someone in my life.

He came back!

"Well, you might as well take off your coat and get comfortable." I walk away, waiting while he does just that and then comes into the living room.

"Who are the flowers from?" he asks.

I tilt my head to the side. "I helped Hannah pick out flowers and cake for the wedding today, and the florist gave them to me."

He nods and lets out a long, slow breath.

"I saw the photo of you with him," he begins, and I frown, watching him start to pace the living room.

"With who?"

"I have no idea who he is," Christian replies with a shrug. "It was posted on one of the gossip sites."

"That's one I haven't seen."

He pulls out his phone, taps it, and then holds it out for me to see.

"Noah," I say softly and hand his phone back. "That's Noah King. He's a good friend of mine. I saw him at Drips & Sips about a week ago."

"I didn't like it. They made it look like you're dating him."

"Yeah? Well, you were splashed all over *Entertainment Tonight* with Serena, and trust me when I say, they didn't make it look like you dislike her. They spin lies, Christian. You know that better than anyone."

"I still didn't like it," he says with a sigh. "And I *do* know how much they love drama. It didn't change the fact that I saw it and wanted to kill him with my bare hands."

"Christian—"

"And I don't know what Nina said to you that day," he continues, on a roll now. "But you need to listen to *me*, not her. She doesn't speak for me, Jenna."

"She didn't lie to me." I stand now, also pacing the room, watching him. We're like two caged animals circling each other. "She didn't say anything that isn't true, Christian. Her delivery might have been a bit harsh, but she's right. We live two *very* different lives. I just don't see how we can make it work. You're movie premieres and fancy houses and cars, and I'm a small-town girl who's happy to take care of vacation rentals and spend my summers on the lake."

I shrug, holding my hands out at my sides. "And, besides, I don't particularly like the press, Christian. I know they're a part of what you do, and it's not your fault, but I hate it. I think it's disrespectful and just plain hurtful the way they target you. They'll always try to pair you with some starlet, to make it look like you're a couple. And even if I know the truth, it doesn't make it easier to live with. I don't know that I can live that life."

"I know." He pushes his hand through his hair and swears under his breath as he walks to the fireplace and shoves his hands into his pockets, watching the flames. "I know what they do, and asking you to take that on isn't fair."

He turns to me now, and his face is full of so much pain, so much anguish, I want to run to him and hold him close, to assure him that everything will be okay.

"They will always do that, Jenna. I can't stop it. Unless…"

His eyes narrow, and he begins walking toward me. "Unless?"

"They won't stop until I put a ring on someone's finger, Jenna. Until I'm finally settled and happy."

He drops to one knee before me, and I feel my eyes widen in shock.

"I'm not saying this for them. I want to make that perfectly clear, right here and now. I've never asked anyone this question before. But, Jenna, I can't do this life without you. I don't think I started to breathe until the moment I first touched you."

He takes my hand and kisses my knuckles, and then reaches into his pocket, pulling out a tiny, red box. He flips the lid, and twinkling at me, is the most amazing ring I've ever seen.

But I can't take my eyes off Christian's face.

"You are the best part of my life, and I will shout that I love you so much that I ache with it from the rooftops without hesitation. I need you by my side for the rest of my life. Let's end this media circus here and now, Jenna. Be mine. Marry me."

I fall to my knees before him and cup his face. I can feel tears flowing down my cheeks, and he brushes them away with his fingers.

"Please," he whispers.

"I love you, too." My voice is soft, and my chest is full of so much joy and hope. "I'm so sorry. I'm so sorry that I pushed you away without trying to talk about all of the conflicting thoughts running through my head. And I'm sorry that I let your sister's words feed my insecurities. You didn't deserve that, and neither did I.

"I fucked up, Christian, and I'm completely honored that you came for me. I would have called you today if you hadn't been here because I've missed you *so much.*"

He smiles and cups my face in his warm hand. "I don't think that this ring is going to stop the media's craziness."

He frowns and opens his mouth to disagree, but I press my fingers to his lips and keep talking. "I think they'll always try to start shit. Your happiness won't be what they want at all, so they'll always find something to stir the pot. But what we need to do is promise to be a team, to just worry about *us* and agree that whatever rumors they start aren't real."

"You're killing me here, Jenna."

"I would be honored to be your wife."

He yanks me into his arms, crushing me in a tight hug, and the next thing I know, his lips are on mine, and we fall to the floor.

He pulls back long enough to get the ring on my finger, and then we're pulling at each other's clothes, anxious to get at each other.

"You'll never regret it," he promises me, kissing his way down my neck to my collarbone. My clothes quickly disappear from my body, and he covers me, pins my hands to the floor, and kisses me until I see stars.

"Mine," he whispers. "You're mine, fancy face."

"Hell, yes, I am." I hitch my leg up over his hip, opening myself to him, and he slides home, making us both gasp in pleasure and relief. "I missed you."

"Oh, baby, I missed you, too."

***

"We still have a lot to talk about," I say an hour later when we're back in our clothes and curled up on the couch. "I don't want to move to L.A."

"I know." He kisses my head and rubs his fingertips up and down my arm. "I'll keep the house there because we'll need to be there sometimes. I do have a job there."

"I realize that, and I'm not asking you to give any of that up. It's going to be a balancing act."

"It's going to take compromise," he replies. "For both of us."

"I can hire a management company to take care of things when we're gone," I say, my wheels already spinning. "But I'll need to be on hand while the park property is being built. I won't leave that to anyone else."

"I understand." He pauses. "I have to be in

Vancouver at the end of February to film Luke's movie. I'm scheduled to be there for five weeks."

"Well, I can come visit. That's not a busy time for me anyway."

"Good. See? We're figuring it out already."

I smile up at him and feel my heart race again at the sight of him. He's heart-stoppingly handsome.

And he's mine.

CHAPTER TWENTY

Christian

SHE SAID YES.

It's the morning after, and I think I'm still in a bit of shock, in the best possible way. Jenna is going to be my wife.

Who knew that would happen when I first came to Montana?

I finish doctoring her coffee, then take both of our mugs to the bedroom where she's sitting up in bed and looking at her phone. The sheets are pulled around her, covering her breasts, but her shoulders are bare. Her blond hair is a bit messy and loose around her clean face.

She's the most beautiful thing I've ever seen in my life.

"I have coffee," I say.

"Awesome, thank you." She doesn't look up, just holds out her hand, but I don't pass it to her right away. She glances up, blinking, and then her eyes focus on the mug and a slow smile spreads over her sexy lips.

"Does this ring make me look engaged?" she reads aloud and then skootches up on her knees, letting the linens fall away from her body as she kisses me soundly. "That's my new favorite mug."

"My hands are full, and I can't touch you."

She smiles against my lips. "I love you." She takes her coffee, rereads the mug, and then takes a sip and settles back into her spot on the bed.

"I kind of love that you're a slow riser." I settle in next to her, sip my own coffee, then open my iPad to read the paper. "Lazy mornings are nice."

"*So* nice," she agrees, taking another sip of her coffee. She's holding it with her left hand and smiles coyly, showing me the message and the ring I chose just for her. "What do you think?"

"I think you're adorable."

The doorbell rings, making us both frown.

"Are you expecting someone?" I ask.

"Nope." She shrugs. "Do you mind answering it? I'm kind of naked here."

"No one gets to see you naked but me." I wink and climb from the bed, throwing on my jeans and a T-shirt, then hurry to the door.

"Is Jenna home?" a young woman asks.

"She is, but she's indisposed at the moment. Can I help you?"

"I'm Brooke. I own Brooke's Blooms, and I have a delivery for her." She holds up a basket and smiles widely. "Would you please pass it on?"

"Happy to. Thanks, Brooke."

She nods and waves as she leaves, and I carry the heavy basket back to the bedroom.

"Whoa. Who sent you that?"

"It's not mine." I set it on the bed in front of her. "Brooke brought it for you."

"Oh, how nice." She opens the card first, and her eyes fly to mine. "This is a hand-written card from your sister."

I cock a brow in surprise. "What does it say?"

Jenna,

I'm so sorry for the way I acted when I was in Montana. I can see now how much you and Christian love each other, and I'm simply thrilled that he proposed. I look forward to getting to know you better, and I hope you can accept my apology.

Congratulations,

Nina

"Well, she still has a ways to go to redeem herself, but this is a start," I say as Jenna starts to rip into the cellophane-wrapped basket. She pulls out girlie things like notebooks and pens, candy in plastic boxes, and a little, potted plant.

"This was very nice of her," Jenna says and sets it all on the floor next to her. She retrieves her coffee and takes a sip. "I have to say, Nina was cruel that day."

"I'm sorry."

"That's not something you need to apologize for, Christian. Nina's an adult. But I guess she's not a total bitch."

"Oh, she can be," I reply with a laugh. "But she loves me, and I think she was trying to protect me. Against what, I'm not sure."

"I'm a sister." She shrugs. "But I don't think I would have done what she did."

"I know you both have a long way to go before you're friends, but I hope that happens eventually. Nina is important to me, and I love her."

She smiles, in that sweet way she does. "We'll work it out."

"You're a good person, Jenna." I settle back into the bed next to her.

"Oh, guess what happened while you were gone?" Jenna asks as she takes another sip of her coffee.

"What's that?"

She sticks out her lower lip in a pout. "Someone bought the property in front of mine on the mountain. I'm afraid I'm about to lose my view."

I clear my throat. "So, I have a confession to make."

She narrows her eyes. "No way."

"I bought it," I confirm. "Part of the charm of your property *is* the view. You can't lose that."

"You didn't have to buy the property for me."

"Yes." I lean over and kiss her lips softly. "I did."

"You're awfully good to me, Mr. Wolfe."

"It's just because I love you, soon-to-be Mrs. Wolfe."

Her cheeks flush as she snorts and sets her mug aside, then reaches for her phone again, typing furiously.

"Who are you chatting with?" I ask.

"It's a group text with Willa, Grace, and Hannah. I *had* to tell them, Christian. I'm sorry, I just couldn't keep it a secret."

"It's not a secret," I reply and lean over to kiss the ball of her shoulder. "Tell everyone. In fact, let's take a selfie with the ring and mug and post it on social media. Post it everywhere. Send me the photo, and I'll do the same."

She's staring at me as if I've just asked her to jump off a cliff. "Don't you have to go through people for announcements like that?"

"Fuck that. This is *my* news, and I say where and when it goes out to the world. This isn't a secret."

She grins and does a little shimmy in the bed, then goes to work smoothing her hair and rubbing her face.

"I don't have any makeup or clothes on."

"You look amazing. Fresh. You're always gorgeous. And we'll keep it rated *G*."

She picks up the mug, positioning it so both it and her ring are pointed toward the camera.

"Now, kiss me," I say and snap the photo when she complies. She turns her face to the camera, and I kiss her cheek and snap another. And then, just for the fun of it, we both smile at the camera, and I take one more. I send all three photos to her. "There, feel free to post any of those."

She looks through them, her face bright with happiness. "They're all cute. But I'll use the one where we're kissing."

"Do it."

She takes a deep breath and stares at me. "Are you sure?"

"Do you want me to do it first?"

She just nods a little, so I pull up my Instagram and post the kissing photo. I caption it #*taken*.

I turn the screen so she can see, and she bites her lip while tears fill her eyes.

"Your turn, fancy face. Unless you want to keep *me* a secret."

"Hell, no." She opens her own Instagram and posts the same thing I just did, then opens her personal Facebook page and uploads the photo of us smiling at the camera. She recites the caption as she types it. "He asked, and I said yes!"

"We should probably turn our ringers off now because they're about to go crazy."

She just laughs and launches herself into my arms.

"I'm crazy about you, movie star."

***

It's been two weeks of craziness. The media had a field day with the announcement of our engagement, and I had to have Nina and my social media team field hundreds of requests for comments and interviews.

I'll give them all a nice bonus for the extra work they've put in.

This evening, we're attending an engagement party that Jacob is hosting for us up at the Lodge on the mountain. I think that half the town came out for it, given that Jenna knows *everyone.*

Nina flew in for it yesterday, and even Luke and Natalie Williams arrived a couple of days ago.

Jenna and I spent the day house hunting with them, and they've decided on a place on the lake. It seems the Williams family will be making many trips to Cunningham Falls in the future.

The food is set up buffet-style so we can all mingle and eat at our own leisure. The room is beautiful with twinkling lights strung overhead and fresh flower bouquets on each table.

Jenna is a few tables away, gorgeous in a white

dress that shows off her shoulders, her hair swept to one side, and her makeup flawless. She's laughing with Grace and Nina, and it makes me happy to see that my sister and my love are mending things between them, one day at a time. Jenna's capacity to forgive is astounding to me.

"Hi," a tall man says as he approaches, and I immediately recognize him from the photo on the gossip site. "I'm Noah King."

"Good to meet you." I shake his hand. "And I need to thank you. If it wasn't for the photo of you hugging Jenna, I might not have come back when I did."

He smiles and looks down at his feet, then at me. "I've never had a hug get me in so much hot water before."

"You're lucky."

"You be good to her. She deserves it."

"You're right. She does."

He nods and walks on, pulling Jenna in for another hug, and this time, I don't even want to slug him.

Progress.

I scan the room, enjoying a free moment to take everything in. Luke and Natalie are talking with Brad and Hannah. I love that everyone here is happy for us as a couple, not because there are celebrities in attendance, and so far, no one has acted like a fool.

It goes to show what I already know, that Cunningham Falls is a community full of respect and honor, and I couldn't be prouder to be a part of it.

Max is standing off to the side, watching Willa intently.

"Careful," I say as I sidle up next to him. "You don't want to be labeled a creeper."

He snorts. "I've been called worse."

"You should go ask her to dance."

He shakes his head no. "There's a lot of history there, man. Too much. Trust me when I say, Willa doesn't want to talk to me, let alone for me to touch her."

I notice Willa glance this way, then quickly avert her gaze to the other side of the room.

"Oh, I don't know about that."

He sighs. "That ship sailed a long time ago. Congratulations. I'm truly happy for you and Jenna."

"Thank you."

"If you fuck it up, Brad and I can still make it look like an accident."

"Understood."

Max winks and walks away, and I wander over to Jacob and shake his hand.

"Thanks so much for hosting this, Jacob."

"Oh, I'm not hosting," he says with a frown. "Your sister planned all of this. I just provided the space."

"She didn't say," I mutter, watching as Nina tells a story to the other girls, using her hands in grand gestures before they all collapse into a fit of giggles.

"She did a *lot* of work," Jacob replies with a wink. "I think I'll go get some dessert."

I nod as he walks away, and I wander over to the DJ, ask him for the mic, and when the music stops, I tap the top of the microphone, getting everyone's attention.

"Good evening," I begin. "First, I need to extend a huge thank you to our host. You went above and beyond, and I can't tell you how grateful I am. Of course, you thought you pulled one over on me, but a brother always knows. Thanks for this party, Nina."

Jenna's jaw drops, and she throws her arms around Nina, hugging her close as the applause breaks out. Nina blushes and just shrugs at me when Jenna pulls away.

"And now, if my fiancée would please join me." I hold out my hand, and Jenna glides to me, her gown flowing around her. She takes my palm, and I immediately kiss her cheek. "I'd like to take a moment to twirl my girl around the floor."

Her eyes widen in horror, but I just smile and pass the mic back to the DJ. He winks at me. *You and I* comes on, and Michael Buble begins to croon out of the speakers. I pull Jenna to me, holding her in the traditional waltz stance.

"Christian—"

"Just look at me," I remind her and set off across the floor. "This is our community. All of these people love you, and you can't do anything to embarrass yourself. All you have to do is follow me, and I won't steer you wrong."

Her hand on my shoulder tenses, but she keeps her eyes on mine as I lead her around, and then dip her deeply, kissing her with all my might.

Applause breaks out around us, making me grin against her mouth.

When we straighten, I wave for others to join us, and the dance floor fills up with our guests, twirling around us.

"I'm not a good dancer," she mumbles into my ear. We're close together now, swaying to the music in a sea of people.

"You're the best dancer." I kiss her temple. "I love our home."

She smiles brightly. "I love *you*."

ABOUT KRISTEN PROBY

Kristen was born and raised in a small resort town in her beloved Montana. In her mid-twenties, she decided to stretch her wings and move to the Pacific Northwest, where she made her home for more than a dozen years.

During that time, Kristen wrote many romance novels and joined organizations such as RWA and other small writing groups. She spent countless hours in workshops, and more mornings than she can count up before the dawn so she could write before going to work. She submitted many manuscripts to agents and editors alike, but was always told no. In the summer of 2012, the self-publishing scene was new and thriving, and Kristen had one goal: to publish just one book. It was something she longed to cross off of her bucket list.

Not only did she publish one book, she's since published more than thirty titles, many of which have hit the USA Today, New York Times and Wall Street Journal Bestsellers lists. She continues to self publish, best known for her With Me In Seattle and Boudreaux series, and is also proud to work with William Morrow, a division of HarperCollins, with the Fusion and Romancing Manhattan Series.

Kristen and her husband, John, make their home in her hometown of Whitefish, Montana with their adorable pug and two cats.

Website

www.kristenproby.com

Facebook

www.facebook.com/BooksByKristenProby

Twitter

twitter.com/Handbagjunkie

Goodreads

goodreads.com/author/show/6550037.Kristen_Proby

Other Books by Kristen Proby

The Big Sky Series

Charming Hannah
Kissing Jenna
Waiting for Willa - Coming Soon

Kristen Proby's Crossover Collection – A Big Sky Novel

Soaring with Fallon
Wicked Force: A Wicked Horse Vegas/Big Sky Novella by Sawyer Bennett
All Stars Fall: A Seaside Pictures/Big Sky Novella by Rachel Van Dyken
Hold On: A Play On/Big Sky Novella by Samantha Young
Worth Fighting For: A Warrior Fight Club/Big Sky Novella by Laura Kaye
Crazy Imperfect Love: A Dirty Dicks/Big Sky Novella by K.L. Grayson
Nothing Without You: A Forever Yours/Big Sky Novella by Monica Murphy

The Fusion Series

Listen To Me
Close To You
Blush For Me
The Beauty of Us
Savor You

The Boudreaux Series

Easy Love
Easy Charm
Easy Melody
Easy Kisses
Easy Magic
Easy Fortune
Easy Nights

The With Me In Seattle Series

Come Away With Me
Under the Mistletoe With Me
Fight With Me
Play With Me
Rock With Me
Safe With Me
Tied With Me
Breathe With Me
Forever With Me

The Love Under the Big Sky Series

Loving Cara
Seducing Lauren
Falling For Jillian
Saving Grace

From 1001 Dark Nights

Easy With You
Easy For Keeps
No Reservations
Tempting Brooke

The Romancing Manhattan Series

All the Way - Coming

ALL THE WAY

A Romancing Manhattan Novel

by Kristen Proby

PROLOGUE

London

"It's about fucking time," my brother, Kyle, snarls from his seat next to me. He's twitchy and mean, both indicative of the drugs coursing through his veins. Although he always had a mean streak. The drugs just make it worse.

"Your sister has been in the hospital and your parents' property had to go through probate," Finn Cavanaugh, my parents' attorney, replies from across the desk. He's a tall man, broad-shouldered in his fancy suit, and his dark hair is short, styled impeccably around his masculine face.

He's much younger than I expected.

"Like I give a shit," Kyle replies, and sends me a sneer. "You're just being a fucking baby."

"Or, you know, I jumped out of a second-story window while my parents burned to death and broke my leg in four places." I shrug and then shake my head and dig my fingertips into my forehead, praying for the incessant pounding there to ease. "I lost everything."

"Drama queen." Kyle rolls his eyes and rubs his dirty fingers over his mouth.

"I can't work," I remind him.

"You're rich."

Same argument, different venue. "I can't dance with this leg, which means I can't work."

"Poor baby," he says, and then lets out a manic laugh. "Who cares? You're getting too fucking old for Broadway anyway. They were about to can your ass. I hope you saved some of that money they've been paying you."

More bullets to my ego, my heart. My head. Because he's not exactly wrong. Thirty-two is old for show business.

But damn it, I love it. And I wanted to leave under my own terms. Not because my parents were killed and I was hurt in the process.

"Let's get to this, shall we?" Finn asks, and slides a bottle of water my way.

"Yeah, let's do it. How much do I get?" Kyle asks, and waits, his eyes pinned on Finn. His foot is bouncing, making that *thump thump thump* noise with each motion, and I want to beat him over the head with my crutch.

"I can read this in its entirety, or—"

"Just get to the fucking chase. What do I get?"

Finn sighs and glances to me, shuts the folder

in front of him, and folds his hands on his desk.

"Kyle, your parents set up a trust for you. You will receive fifteen hundred dollars per month to cover your rent and utilities, with the stipulation that you enter drug rehabilitation and finish the program. After one year of sobriety, and with regular clean blood tests, the trust will award you a lump sum of fifty thousand dollars each year until your death."

"What?"

I glance at Kyle and see that his face has gone bright red with fury.

"If you refuse treatment, you forfeit any and all inheritance."

Kyle's mouth bobs open and closed for several seconds, and then he turns to me, royally pissed off.

"Did you do this?"

"Like I had any idea what Mom and Dad put in their will." I roll my eyes and grip my hands in fists in my lap while Kyle stands and begins pacing the room. "You may want to call security."

Finn nods and presses a button while he continues to watch Kyle. He looks calm, but his jaw twitches, and I can see that he's angry at Kyle's behavior as well.

"What does she get?" Kyle demands, pointing at my head.

"Everything else," Finn replies simply. "Your

father's partnership in his firm will be sold. London inherits the properties and all of the other monies."

"Are you fucking kidding me?" Kyle roars, leaning over Finn's desk. "She stole my money! That belongs to *me*! She has plenty of her own goddamn money. What am I supposed to do? I have *nothing* because those people wouldn't help me, and now I'm left with nothing again?"

"No, you can take the option of getting help," Finn reminds him, but I just shake my head. That's not going to happen. We've been trying to do this for *years*. "The rehab would be paid for, and you can stay there until you feel confident that you're ready to rejoin society."

"Bullshit," Kyle bites out, and sweeps all of Finn's papers off of his desk in one big motion. "I should kick your motherfucking ass."

"Enough!" I yell just as three security guards come inside and take him by the arms to escort him out.

"This is bullshit," he repeats as he's dragged down the hallway. The door closes behind them, but I can still hear him yelling.

Finn and I sit in silence for a long moment. I wish my leg wasn't broken because I'd love to stand and walk to the windows that look out over Manhattan. Mostly, I'd like to turn away from Finn so he can't see the absolute anguish on my face.

I'm an actress. A Tony Award–winning one, at that, but I just can't hide my feelings today.

"I'm sorry," I say at last, and clear my throat. "As you can see, my brother isn't well."

Finn doesn't say anything, he just reaches for his phone and calls his assistant. "Please bring in some hot tea."

He hangs up and watches me in silence until the tea arrives. He pours us each a cup and passes one to me, along with sweetener and milk, and when we both have our tea the way we like it, he says, "Do I have to worry about him coming after you to hurt you?"

I glance up in surprise. "He doesn't know where I live."

He pins me with those chocolate-brown eyes. "Do you honestly believe that?"

I take a sip of my Earl Grey and then sigh. "No. I'm sure he could find me. My building is secure. I'm not worried about him."

"I can file a restraining order."

I laugh. "For what? A piece of paper isn't going to stop him if he gets it in his head to find and hurt me." I shake my head and take another sip of tea. "No, I've dealt with him and his issues most of my life. He'll disappear for a while now, do God knows what, until he runs out of money again and calls me."

"Do you give him money?"

"Not anymore." I squirm in my seat and then set my tea aside. "Thanks for the tea, but I'm okay. We can finish this."

Finn opens the folders and passes me forms to sign, explaining how the properties will be transferred to my name.

"You're a very wealthy woman, London."

"I was wealthy before this," I reply, hearing the hollowness in my voice. "I didn't need my parents to die in order to have money."

"Of course not," he says, shaking his head. "I meant no disrespect."

My leg is beginning to ache again. I've only been taking the bare minimum of the pain meds, unwilling to be in a constant hazy coma. But damn, it hurts today.

"If we're finished, I'll go."

"Can I give you a ride home?" he asks, standing with me. I reach for my crutches and get myself situated.

"I have a car and driver."

He nods and shoves his hands in his pockets. "Can I take you to dinner?"

I glance up in surprise. Finn's a sexy man, and under normal circumstances, I'd do more than let him buy me dinner.

But these aren't normal circumstances.

"Seriously?" I tip my head to the side and scowl at him, no longer surprised, and fully irritated. "You're asking me out just after you've read my parents' will?"

He rubs his fingers over his mouth and then

shakes his head, as if he's at a loss for words, and escorts me out to the elevator. "Just call if you have any questions or need anything at all."

"I have one question. Now that I own all of the properties, can I live in them?"

"Of course."

I step into the elevator, turn to face him, and offer him a small smile. "Thanks."

CHAPTER 1

London

Three months a year. That's how much time I spent here on Martha's Vineyard off the coast of Massachusetts each summer of my entire life. The rest of the year we lived in Connecticut, so my brother and I could go to school and do what families do.

But every summer, from the day after school let out until the day before we went back, my family lived here, on the beach in the West Chop area of the island. Our house is massive, and worth several million dollars, but as a child, I didn't know that. I just knew that it was a magical place of sunshine and water, of summertime friends that came back every year. Of daydreams and happiness.

It was more home to me than our "full-time" house then, and it still is.

So when Finn told me two months ago that I had inherited all of my parents' properties, and that

I could live in them or do what I wished with them, I knew that I'd come here for the summer.

Home.

I'm walking on the beach, without a cane now, thank you very much, enjoying the breeze from the ocean. I have over a hundred feet of private beach, but I can hear kids playing off in the distance, and sailboats are gently meandering by with bright sails and happy people.

At least, they're happy in my head.

Walking in the sand isn't as easy as I would like. My leg aches like a toothache, but it's healing. Slower than I'd like, but it's getting there.

The sand is warm beneath my bare feet, and I have to hold my dark hair off of my face as I stop and look out at the choppy water.

"Because I just have to be meeeee . . ."

I glance over my shoulder at the sound of the small voice and smile. A little girl with a riot of dark curls is dancing down the beach, making grand gestures with her arms and singing loudly. Ironically, she's singing the song from the musical that I starred in for over a year on Broadway.

She stops when she sees me and glances around like she's not quite sure how she got here.

"You have a pretty voice," I say kindly.

"Thanks," she says, and shrugs one shoulder. She's tall, but I don't know kids well enough to know if she's tall for her age. Her eyes are sky blue, standing out against her olive skin and dark hair. "It's my favorite musical."

I nod, smiling. "Mine too."

"Is that your house?" she asks, pointing behind me.

"It is," I confirm. "Where do you live?"

"Over there," she says with a sigh, pointing to the house next to mine. "But ours doesn't have a pool or a playhouse like yours."

I tilt my head to the side, watching her. "You must have had a look around, since I don't think you can see all of that from your house."

She shrugs one shoulder again. "Yeah. I guess."

"Gabby!" A man comes running down the beach, a scowl on his face. "You know this isn't our beach. You can't just run off like that."

Gabby rolls her eyes and then turns back to him, and as he gets closer, I immediately recognize him.

Finn Cavanaugh.

"I'm right here," she says.

"Hey," he says to me, and offers me a small smile. "Sorry if she was bothering you."

Gabby rolls her eyes again, and I can't help but laugh a little. "She's not bothering me at all. We were talking about musicals."

His lips twitch, and I'm reminded just how handsome Finn is. Scratch that. Not handsome.

Fucking hot.

Just my luck, he's my neighbor.

Which I knew, I just forgot.

"How are you feeling?" he asks as Gabby twirls in a circle and dances away to sing and dance some more.

"Better," I reply. "Not fantastic, but I'm finally rid of the crutches and cane, so I'll take it."

"You look good," he says, and then clears his throat. "Any issues?"

Oh, you know, my parents are dead and have left me with a mess to clean up all by myself, my leg is killing me, and I'm pretty sure I lost my career, but nothing major.

"No, I'm good."

He watches me for a moment and then nods. His hands are in his pockets the same way they were in his office two months ago, but this time he's not wearing a suit. No, he's in a red T-shirt and black cargo shorts with no shoes.

I had no idea the casual look could be sexier than the suit, but here we are.

"Your daughter is beautiful."

He grins and glances at Gabby, then turns back to me. "She's my niece. She's staying with me for about a month."

"Oh, that's nice."

He frowns and looks down, and I feel like I've

said the wrong thing, but the moment passes and he calls over to Gabby, "It's about time for your horse-riding lesson, Gabs. We should go."

"Fine," she replies with a heavy sigh, and takes off running toward his house.

"She doesn't like horses?" I ask.

"She does, she's just been difficult lately, so very little makes her particularly happy. It's a long story."

"Well, I don't want to keep you." I step back and offer him a smile. "Oh, before you go, it finally clicks as to why you represented my parents. You're the neighbor."

"I've spent the past five summers here," he confirms. "I liked your parents very much. Your dad asked me to update his will about two years ago."

I nod. "Makes sense. Have a good day."

"You too, London."

And with that, he turns and jogs down the beach back to his own house, which is only about a hundred yards from mine. His shoulders are ridiculously broad, especially from behind.

And speaking of behinds, his ass is something to write home about.

Or something to grip on to while he fucks a girl silly.

I clear my throat and shake my head as I walk back toward my house. I must be feeling better if

I'm undressing the sexy neighbor with my eyes. I'm not irritated with him anymore for asking me out on that day at his office. That doesn't mean that it wasn't inappropriate. Because it was.

But on a scale of one to house fires on the life-altering scale, that would be a negative fourteen.

I walk up the sandy path to the house, brush my feet clean, and walk inside through the screened sun porch to the kitchen. I brewed some iced tea this morning, so I pour myself a glass, add some lemon, and carry it with me to the library, where I've been working all morning on sorting books.

Mom loved to read. She has to have more than a thousand books in here, everything from out-dated encyclopedias to paperback romance novels. Thrillers, true crime, interior design, and biographies are in there too.

And pretty much everything else.

I remember when we'd come here in the summer, I'd be playing at the beach or in the pool with friends, and Mom would be on the sun porch with a book and a glass of tea, absorbed in another world, but ready for us in case we needed anything.

I sit at her desk and take a sip of my tea before carefully placing it on a coaster and reaching for another stack of books.

Some of them are signed by the authors, so it's not just a matter of donating the ones that I won't read or don't need. I have to look at every single one of them, check for a signature, notes or thoughts that Mom might have written in them, pressed flowers, you name it.

It's become a long process.

I have two boxes nearby. One for donations and one for trash. I mean, who needs an encyclopedia from 1987? Not me. That's what Google is for. And there are plenty of books that are empty and would be welcome at a library or the Goodwill.

Just as I toss a paperback into a box, my phone pings with a text.

What are you doing? It's from Sasha, a former colleague and my best friend. She's in New York, working on a new play that debuts in six weeks, but she texts or calls every single day, checking in on me.

Sorting books in the library. What are you doing?

I set the phone aside, take a sip of my tea, and glance out the window as a huge sailboat with a bright-blue sail soars past.

Having lunch before I head back to rehearsal. Are you ready to sort through your parents' things? They haven't been gone long.

I smile at her concern. She's always been a mother hen.

I can't just sit in this big house and do nothing. I might as well get something accomplished. It's just the library.

Not their bedroom, or the kitchen, where

Mom's special dishes are. Those two rooms will have to wait for quite some time.

Don't overdo it. When is your next PT?

Now I feel like Gabby when I roll my eyes and reply.

Tomorrow. Go to rehearsal and stop harassing me.

I grin and rub my thigh where it's started to ache again. I'll take more Advil when I go downstairs.

Fine. You're so difficult. Call you later!

I shove my phone in my pocket, and now that I've gone through that stack of books, I decide to go downstairs rather than reach for more. They're heavy, and I'm tired. One thing I've learned during this whole damn mess is to listen to my body and not push it too hard. If I'm tired, I need to nap. If I hurt, I need to take something. Being miserable isn't worth being stubborn.

I hobble slowly down the stairs to the kitchen and take two Advil, and then wander to my favorite napping spot on the porch. I'll let the ocean breeze lull me to sleep.

***

I don't know what the fuck I'm doing.

I'm standing in my driveway, the hood of my car open, and I'm staring at it as if it just magically holds all of the answers.

So far, all I see is a bunch of stuff that I know

absolutely nothing about.

All I do know for sure is, the damn car won't start.

"Don't do this to me today," I plead with the three-year-old BMW. "I have to go to PT today, and I'm already running late. Please start."

With that, I march around to the driver's side, prop my ass on the seat, and push the start button.

Nothing.

"What the hell?"

I get out and face the open engine again, frowning as if it's scorned me on purpose.

"Okay, maybe Siri knows." I pull the app up on my phone and speak into it. "Siri, my BMW won't start. Can you diagnose the problem?"

"I'm sorry, I don't understand."

I roll my eyes and try again.

"Why won't my BMW start?"

She thinks for a second. "I can't find that answer."

I groan and then try again.

"Siri, please give me possible reasons for why my BMW engine won't start."

"You should seek a professional."

I close my eyes and take a deep breath. "Yeah, no shit. Why are you always such a bitch to me, Siri?"

I hear movement behind me and startle when I see Finn standing there, his hands on his lean hips and a smirk on that sexy face of his.

"How long have you been there?"

"Long enough to hear you have an argument with Siri."

"I thought this was a *smart* phone." I wag it in the air. "If that's the case, wouldn't she know what's going on?"

"In theory. Maybe someday they'll be that smart."

I sigh and turn back to the car. "I guess I'll call AAA."

"Well, hold on. What's wrong?"

"It won't start. It doesn't even make a noise. Just . . . *nothing.*"

He steps up beside me and glances inside. Suddenly he reaches in and wiggles something around.

"Try it again."

"Seriously, I can call someone."

"London." He looks down at me with hot brown eyes now and leans both hands on the car, as if he's keeping himself from touching me.

Which is completely all in my head and wishful thinking because he's a stranger and I've been without sex for way too long.

"Yeah?"

"Try it again."

"Okay, I'll humor you, but I really think it's something far more serious than that." I prop my ass on the seat again and push the button, and just like that, the car comes to life. "What did you do?"

"The cable to the battery was loose, which is odd, but not impossible, I guess. It should be fine now."

"Thanks." I check the time and swear under my breath. "I'm late, and they won't see me now. I'll have to reschedule my appointment."

"So you're free for a while?" he asks, and I look up to find him smiling at me.

"Depends."

"Well, how about if I take you to lunch?"

"If you're going to feed me, yes, I'm free." I smile and then blink, remembering that he showed up out of nowhere. "Wait. Why did you come over here?"

"I was walking out to my own car and heard you talking to Siri," he says with a shrug. "I wasn't trying to be nosy, but I figured you could use a hand."

"Thanks."

He nods. "So, lunch?"

"Where's Gabby?"

"I have to pick her up from piano lessons. She'll join us, if that doesn't bother you."

"That doesn't bother me."

"Great." He waits for me to follow him over to his car, opens the door for me, and pulls out of his driveway.

"So, Gabby had horseback-riding lessons yesterday, and piano lessons today?"

"Yes," he says with a nod. "I have her in several activities. I want her to meet other kids and have fun."

"I don't mean to pry, but is she okay?"

He sighs and signals to make a turn. "I'm not sure what's up with her. She's been really challenging for her dad, so I offered to bring her here for a few weeks to give him a break. I was hoping it would help her attitude, but so far it hasn't."

"Where's her mom?"

"She passed away about five years ago," he replies. "Her mom was my younger sister. Carter, Gabby's dad, is still a good friend, and a partner at the firm, and he was about at his wit's end with her."

"Maybe she's just going through a rough patch."

He nods and swings into a driveway where Gabby is waiting on the porch of a house with a grandmotherly woman waiting with her. She waves at Finn as Gabby runs down to the car.

"She's in my seat," she grumbles as she climbs into the backseat.

"London is my guest and you'll be polite, young

lady," Finn says, staring her down in the rearview mirror. "Apologize for being rude."

"Sorry," she says, and looks out her window as Finn pulls out of the driveway. He takes us to a restaurant by the water that is known for its fish and chips.

"I love this place," I say when he finds a space to park. "I've come here since I was a kid."

"Perfect," he says with a smile, and we all climb out of the car and get settled at a table inside. Once we've ordered our lunch and have our drinks, I take a sip of lemonade and turn to Gabby.

"So, what musicals are your favorite, Gabby?"

"*A Summer's Evening* is my favorite," she says, not looking me in the eyes.

"Really? That's the musical that I acted in for a few years."

She nods. "Yeah, I know. My dad took me a couple of times."

She shrugs a shoulder, like it's no big deal. Which is fine with me.

"Uncle Finn has me in those stupid piano lessons, but I'd rather learn how to sing better."

I glance up at Finn. "Well, I can give you voice lessons."

Her eyes fly up to mine, holding a little bit of hope now. "You could?"

"Sure." I shrug, as if it's no big deal, mimicking her movement from a few seconds ago, and wink at

Finn. "I mean, I've taken voice and dance since I was a little girl. I could totally help you."

She clears her throat and then nods. "Yeah, that could be cool."

"Okay, well, when it works with your schedule, we'll do that."

Our food is delivered, and I dig in, suddenly realizing that I'm starving. The meal is full of fat and oil. Tons of carbs. And I don't even care.

When my basket is empty, I sit back and pat my food belly. "Good lord, that was good. What did you think, Gabby?"

"Pretty good," she admits, and gives Finn the side-eye, not wanting to show too much enthusiasm.

"Thanks for inviting me along. What do you guys have planned for the rest of the day?"

"Gabby has her first karate lesson," Finn says, and my head spins. Good God, she goes nonstop, and it's her summer vacation.

"You're a busy girl."

"Tell me about it," she says, rolling her eyes again. "I thought we would come here to relax, I mean, school's out and all, but Uncle Finn has me doing *everything*."

"I don't want you to be bored," he says, and nudges her with his elbow, but she scoots away from him. She doesn't see the look of hurt in his eyes, and I feel badly for him.

"There are a ton of fun things to do here," I reply. "Have you thought of sailing lessons?"

"I don't like the water," she says, shaking her head.

"Okay. Well, I think karate sounds fun."

She just shrugs again and looks out the window, ignoring us both now.

"What about you?" Finn asks me. "What do you have planned?"

"Well, thanks to my car, I missed my PT appointment, so I'll have to reschedule that. I was going to do some baking this evening."

"What are you making?" Gabby asks.

"Pies. Maybe some cookies. I'll bring you guys some. I love to bake, but I can't eat any of it."

"None of it?" Gabby asks with wide eyes.

"Nope, I have to stay in shape for my job."

I blink rapidly, realizing that I probably *don't* have a job to stay in shape for, but I don't say that. Staying in good physical condition is a habit, and even if I don't get to dance onstage again, it's a healthy habit to have.

"I love pie," Gabby says with a bright smile.

"I thought you might."